MW01233175

Out Of Darkness

A Novel By

Melba Conaway

AuthorHouse™
1663 Liberty Drive
Bloomington, IN 47403
www.authorhouse.com
Phone: 1-800-839-8640

First published by AuthorHouse 1/26/2011

ISBN: 978-1-4567-2189-3 (sc)
ISBN: 978-1-4567-2190-9 (hc)
ISBN: 978-1-4567-2191-6 (e)

Library of Congress Control Number: 2010919594

Printed in the United States of America

This book is printed on acid-free paper.

Introduction

Out of Darkness Into Light

". . . that ye should show forth the praises of him who hath called you out of darkness into his marvelous light." 1 Peter 2:9b

May this story be a form of praise to our Heavenly Father who has shed His light into my soul, my daily life, and provided physical sight that I feared was gone forever.

May God open your eyes to see His marvelous works in your own life.

This is my prayer for the story and for the reader.

~ Prologue ~

Long ago, and far away – it was an entirely different life.

I was a happy little girl, growing up in a happy little family in the pleasant little town of Maplesville, Missouri. Maplesville was a typical small town of the times. It had a thriving main street, the usual schools and the required number of churches. It was also the home of the area community college where my father taught as a professor of mathematics.

During the early 50's, when I was born, our community seemed sheltered and protected from the crises and crime of the larger world. During my childhood, even during my high school years, no catastrophe greater than having to miss Marcy's birthday party because of chicken pox, marred my pleasant, serene life. To say I was unprepared for what lay ahead was the proverbial understatement.

During all those years, my world revolved around ME, -- my needs, my desires. My mother was my confidant and best friend. But with her death following my graduation from high school, my life changed completely. The world no longer adapted to my needs and whims. I had to face it all alone.

Trusting in my own strength and wisdom, I made some tragic mistakes. But through it all, denied and ignored by me, the Great God of the Universe was molding and making me into His will. The things that happened to me and my reaction to them, do not make a "happy little story." But I hope that, as you read, and feel the things I experienced. Your understanding of me and these events will enable you to see the Hand of God in your own life.

Chapter One

I am so tired and discouraged. There's nothing more frustrating than trying to work in the dark.

Oh, I'm not really in the dark, -- exactly. In fact, the fixture that hangs over my workspace holds a 300 watt bulb. The trouble seems to be with my eyes -- or my right eye, specifically. What can I do? How can I sketch when I can't see what I did just a moment ago? I suppose it's my own fault. I should have made another appointment with the ophthalmologist when I wasn't able to keep the first one. Now the cataract must be getting worse.

But how could I think of eyes during such a difficult time? When my world fell apart and there was no where to turn for comfort or help, going to see a doctor was the least of my problems.

I wouldn't even be here at work today, except work has always been my salvation. When Mr. Whitman gave me the special commission to design an exclusive line of career apparel in time for the fall and winter showing, I jumped at the chance. It will require a lot of work, original ideas and concentration. When I'm involved in the work, I don't think about sadness, grief or feelings.

Actually, I am very fortunate to have such a good position. I'm Angela Graham. Yes, THE Angela, whose name you have seen on the labels of the exclusive designs from the famous Baker House, one of the largest houses of design for women's apparel in the country. Here, in St. Louis, we set the standard for fashion. In fact our designs influence the markets in New York, Dallas, Los Angeles and other fashion centers.

As I say, I'm fortunate. Yet it is just a part of my plan for my life. Just out of high school, I soon realized I must be able to depend on myself, alone, in this cruel world. In order to do that, I needed money. A lot of money.

Since I had a little artistic ability, and a definite sense of what is "right" and "smart" in fashion, this was the best way to get it.

I studied at the prestigious New York University of Art and Design. When I completed my course, I looked for the best opportunity to get into the field and begin making money.

Being successful really wasn't the only thing I wanted. I wanted a husband – the right husband. And I found him!

~ ~ ~ ~ ~ ~ ~ ~ ~ ~ ~ ~ ~

One morning, about three years ago, I stopped by Mr. Whitman's (he's my boss) office to deliver some rough sketches, and literally bumped into this handsome young fellow that seemed to draw me like a magnet. He was about six feet tall with dark, wavy hair, cut long in the back, but shaped nicely on the sides and top. And those startling brown eyes! Yes, brown eyes. I have always been partial to brown eyes. Mine are blue, --nice enough, I guess. And they go with my long, blonde hair. But brown eyes have always done something special for me.

"I'm so sorry," I stammered.

"It's my fault. Should watch where I'm going. Please forgive me. Are you all right?"

I couldn't help but stare into that handsome face as I muttered, "Yes, of course."

He was embarrassed. "Chuck Graham, ma'am. At your service."

I grinned as I shook his outstretched hand. "Angela Dobson." (That was my maiden name.)

Then he was gone.

But that was just the beginning. It wasn't too difficult to learn that Chuck Graham was actually Charles David Graham, an enterprising advertising executive with a prestigious local firm. Our paths began to cross more frequently as Chuck's firm took over more and more of the advertising for Baker House.

As we worked together, we soon realized that, most of the time, we looked at things from the same angle. When we did disagree, we were usually able to work out an acceptable compromise. Actually, we were just good together.

So one thing led to another, and soon we were married. It was a real story book marriage. Oh, how my heart aches, as I remember. We were completely in love. We both made good money and were able to afford the nice things we wanted. I guess you could say we were the typical "yuppies." Everything was going our way. We were on top of the world and nothing could stop us. And we did it all by ourselves. We didn't need family, or friends, or anyone outside ourselves.

We were completely sufficient for each other. Life was good.

The only problem, and it was a minor one, was that I began having some difficulty in seeing my work, especially at night. Chuck was concerned and had insisted that I have an examination for glasses or contacts. My concern was in having to wear glasses. Glasses were for old people. After all, I was only 24 and I didn't want to ruin my looks with glasses.

However, it didn't turn out to be quite that simple. The optometrist suspected cataracts and made an appointment for me with Dr. Kenneth Wallace, a noted ophthalmologist. I didn't keep that appointment. It was two weeks away, and I put it out of my mind, and began making plans for the weekend.

Both of us had been working pretty hard and deserved some time off. We would go to the mountains. We got the reservations and planned to leave as soon as Chuck got home Friday afternoon. We would come back late Sunday night. Two glorious days away from the "rat race."

~ ~ ~ ~ ~ ~ ~ ~ ~ ~ ~ ~ ~

But Chuck was late. That was so unlike him. I was afraid we might miss our plane if he didn't show up soon. Maybe he got caught in the rush hour traffic, but even so, he should have been home by now.

Just when I had about given up hope of getting to the airport on time, the door bell rang. Ah, maybe he forgot his key.

When I opened the door, it wasn't Chuck, but a uniformed policeman who said, "Mrs. Graham?"

"Yes," I almost whispered. "What's wrong?" But I knew, deep in the cold, empty place in my stomach, even before he answered. Something had happened to Chuck.

"There's been a serious accident involving your husband's car. Could you come with me to the hospital?"

"Of course," I said, as I grabbed my purse and followed him to his cruiser.

The ride to the hospital was brief. But it didn't matter. Chuck was already gone before we got there.

Gone? Chuck dead? It couldn't be. He was too alive. and so young. I just couldn't take it all in. My mind refused to accept it.

Someone kept trying to tell me something about a freak accident -- how another car had slammed into Chuck, and he had been crushed, as his car turned over and rolled. He didn't have a chance.

I really didn't understand it exactly. But it didn't matter. My life was over. Without Chuck, everything was gone.

Chapter Two

I didn't know what to do. I couldn't even think.

Instinctively, I called my Father. I don't know why I did. It just seemed to be the thing to do.

Of course, my father came immediately. He had always supported me whenever I let him. I was the "baby" of the family, with an older sister and two brothers. Maybe that was the reason I seemed to be his favorite, although, actually, I believe he loved all his children equally. But when Mother died about the time I graduated from high school, I was the only child still at home. That may be why he was so protective.

At any rate, I had always known he was there and I suppose we could have had a close relationship. But I really didn't have time. Like I said, I had to get out in the world and seek my fortune. Dad paid all my bills when I went to New York and I thanked him. But I just didn't have time for any "father -- daughter" act.

I've been pretty independent since Mother's death. That really cut me to the quick. Just when I needed her, she was gone.

But Dad had this phobia about trusting in the Lord and He would take care of you. I hated to argue with him. He IS my father. But it was plain to me that God didn't always take care of us. In fact, I thought He was pretty unfair. We had always gone to church and did the things we were supposed to do.

Yet, God took my mother while she was still a young woman and I needed her so.

I found it hard to accept her death and it didn't help to pretend that God was going to make it easier. There was only one thing for me to do.

Get away. And become the person I wanted to be, the person I was capable of being.

Dad and I were on friendly terms, I guess you might say, but we didn't see each other much. My brothers and sister didn't seem to understand me, either. After Chuck and I were married, I, more or less, lost track of everyone. I didn't need anyone else.

But now, I called Dad. Out of force of habit, I guess. And all of the family came; Doris, the big sister who always took care of me when I was little; Warren and Darren, my brothers; and Betty Jean, Darren's wife, my best friend when we were growing up. Some of Chuck's family were there, too. But I don't remember who they were.

I probably wouldn't have made it to the funeral if Doris hadn't taken me in hand and led me around. I really don't recall anything that happened then, or for several days, for that matter.

I guess everyone went home except Dad. I suppose he thought I needed him. I do remember Dr. Wright, a friend of the pastor at home, stopping by one day. But he may have come to visit with Dad. They had a long conversation before he left.

~ ~ ~ ~ ~ ~ ~ ~ ~ ~ ~ ~ ~

One morning, about a week after the funeral, Dad said he would like to see our studio. It was a spacious room with a skylight, located on the second floor of the house.

This was the heart of our home. Chuck and I both worked here whenever we had time or needed to get some extra work done. It was good to share ideas. And we had good times there. After a spell of work, we would often stop for a snack, then find ourselves laughing and talking together and drawing the warm cloak of our marriage around us.

When Dad went upstairs with me, he asked which easel was Chuck's. I pointed it out and sat on his stool. My mind was blank.

I have no idea how long I sat there, staring at the unfinished work. Suddenly I realized I was holding his pencil -- Chuck's pencil. The one he had used to make those sketches. The one he would never use again. Something snapped. I began to cry. I hadn't been able to before. Things began to sort themselves out in my mind.

But, oh, how it hurt! A part of me wanted to say it wasn't true. Chuck would come home any minute and things would be as they had always been. As I began to think more clearly, I knew I had to accept reality. But, right then, I couldn't think of any way to handle it.

Then I remembered Dad. He wasn't there. He must have stepped out some time ago. I had better find him and tell him I had come back to earth.

"Thanks, Dad, for standing by," I said when I found him in the kitchen puttering with sandwich stuff.

"Of course, my child. It was all I could do. But it was what I wanted to do. If there was only some way I could take this from you, I would really give my life to do it."

His tenderness touched me so, and I clung to him, crying again.

After a while, when I was calmer, and we had eaten the sandwiches, Dad said we should talk about practical things. There was that real world that I had tried to blot out.

So we decided to accept the insurance adjuster's suggestion to total Chuck's car. I really didn't need another car. Then we completed the forms to file for Chuck's life insurance. And I remembered again -- the day Chuck told me about the policy, how large it was, and the amount of premiums. We had calculated that the company would make a lot more off of us in the next fifty years than they would have to pay out later. We had laughed about it. Never did I expect to collect so soon. And the tears came again.

~ ~ ~ ~ ~ ~ ~ ~ ~ ~ ~ ~ ~

The next few days are still kind of a blur to me. I soon realized I wouldn't need such a large house, so I called a realtor. Fortunately, there had been mortgage insurance so anything I realized from the sale could be used to buy a more suitable place.

As I taking care of all the details that surrounded an unexpected death, I asked for a little time off from work. I never knew when grief would raise its ugly head. Just when I thought I was doing so well, suddenly, I would be crying again.

~ ~ ~ ~ ~ ~ ~ ~ ~ ~ ~ ~ ~

I guess Dad thought he was trying to help. But he kept suggesting that I pray and trust the Heavenly Father to help me carry my grief. I tried to be polite. He had been so good and kind. But eventually I got all I could take.

"Dad, stop it! I can't stand any more. You have been kind and helpful. But, please, don't talk to me about God at a time like this. You know how I feel about that. You remember what we went through when Mother died. It was then that I knew that, if a God existed, He certainly didn't care about people. Chuck's death has not changed my mind. Don't you see? I picked up the pieces and made a whole new life for myself. Now that's gone, too. If God exists, he must take pleasure in crushing people. How can I trust him? I want no part of your God."

"You've been a big help, Dad. I don't know how I would have made it without you. But now it's time for you to go home to your own life. Don't worry. I'll be fine. I'm stronger. Heartier now. I'll find a way to live with this, as I did before. I don't need your God or any other crutch to lean on. I have strength and ability, and I'll make it on my own."

Dad looked a little shocked. Yes, even sad. He didn't seem to know what to say. It was almost as if he had given up on me. But I sensed he hadn't given up on his God, and he would probably keep praying for me just like he always had.

But he did go home. I promised to write or call. It was a tearful good-bye as we went our separate ways.

Chapter Three

So here I am -- back at work. Because I didn't know what else to do, I guess. And when I can get absorbed in this project, I'll, at least, have a few hours without having to think, to remember, to hurt.

I wish I could see a little clearer, but these are only the rough first sketches. I'll do much better later. They will help get my thinking into focus and give a little direction to my planning. I need to take another trip through the art museum where they display the physical history of the Old West. There are some lines and colors that I can use to advantage. Maybe over the weekend.

But right now, I guess I had better call that doctor's office and see if I can get another appointment. I hate to be slowed down like this. I have a life to rebuild.

The receptionist was nice enough when I told her why I didn't keep my appointment, and she seemed glad to make another. But I've got to wait two weeks. That's a long time to fight this battle. She just doesn't realize how important this is to me.

~ ~ ~ ~ ~ ~ ~ ~ ~ ~ ~ ~ ~

I liked Dr. Wallace the minute I walked into his office. He gave me a firm handshake and a nice smile.

As he placed me in the chair and adjusted the equipment, we talked about the weather. Finally he asked about my work and I explained how important it was that I be able to see perfectly.

"Let's just have a look," he said, as he adjusted the head piece of the instrument to my face. Then he asked me to lean slightly forward and stare at his right ear lobe.

He seems to be taking a rather long time, but then, maybe I'm just impatient. I like his thoroughness. He's a man that inspires confidence.

At last, he straightens up, pushes the instrument away, and tells me to get more comfortable. I can see he is about to give me a lecture, but I want him to understand how I feel too.

I didn't like the sound of the word, "cataract," when Dr. White, the optometrist, mentioned it earlier. But I have had so much difficulty lately, that I shall really be glad to get it taken care of.

"I understand that cataracts aren't the big problem they used to be."

"Yes, that's right," said Dr. Wallace, thoughtfully. "Anything that deals with our eyesight must be taken seriously, and new techniques have made cataract surgery much more simple and successful. However, I didn't find any indication that you have a cataract in either eye."

"Well, that's wonderful, Doctor. I'm really relieved to hear that. Just some glasses, I guess, should fix things up. I really hate to wear glasses. But that's false pride. Or, maybe you could prescribe contacts?"

"Slow down, just a minute, young lady. What I said was that you don't appear to have cataracts. I'm afraid it's not that simple. I see strong indications in both eyes, but especially in the right, of a much more serious problem."

He picked up a large model of the human eye, touching each part as he talked. "You see, your eyes are like cameras. They focus on the picture which is transmitted back to the optic nerve. If the lens of your camera became marred or scratched, we could remove the old one and replace it with a new, clear lens. But if the film is frayed or fuzzy, we still get a poor picture -- maybe even no picture at all. Can you understand that?"

"Why, yes, I think so, Doctor. But what does that have to do with me? Are you saying my film is fuzzy?" I couldn't help a nervous laugh.

"Well, something like that. This problem has a name -- Macular Degeneration." He writes the words on a slip of paper and hands it to me. "This is a situation that we don't know much about. Once it begins to progress, there seems to be no stopping it."

"Wait a minute, Doctor. What does this mean? Why do I have this problem? What can you do about it? Will I be off work long? Give me a little more detail, please."

"To begin with, we really don't know why anyone has this problem. Various theories have been put forth -- genetic or injury. But, actually, nothing has been conclusive. It just happens to some people and not to others. Age, may be a factor in some cases, but gender seems to have nothing to do with it. As for treatment, there is nothing that has proved effective."

Dr. Wallace explained further, "Two types of this disease have been discovered, "wet" and "dry." The "dry" type seems to be more stable, perhaps deteriorating at a slower rate. Your problem however, is the "wet" kind that sometimes has a tendency to "leak" and needs to be sealed. This will require my seeing you on a regular basis to monitor the situation. Now, not everyone reacts in the same way. In some people, the problem is very slow in developing, sometimes taking years. In others, once the degeneration begins, it happens very quickly."

"But let me offer you a word of encouragement," the doctor continued. "In most cases this does not result in complete blindness. Peripheral vision remains. That means that while you may not be able to see directly ahead, as in reading, etc., you will still be able to see daylight and find your way in familiar surroundings."

Dr, Wallace tried to calm my fears. "Now, I know this is a shock to you and you will need some time to think about it. I'll ask my receptionist to make another appointment for you for a week from today. Come back then, and let's reexamine your eyes and answer whatever questions that may have occurred to you by then. This is a rather common complaint and many other people have learned to deal with it. You appear to be a very capable and determined person. I'm sure you can handle it. I want you to know that I am available to help in any way I can. See you next week."

He shakes my hand, helps me to my feet and ushers me out the door.

I'm sitting here, in my car, with my head in my hands, trying to take it all in. But all I can think of is, 'I'm going blind!'

Guess I had better try to make it home, to the new house, while I can still find the way. After I change my clothes, I'll get a sandwich. That should help.

~ ~ ~ ~ ~ ~ ~ ~ ~ ~ ~ ~

It didn't help much, as I lie wide awake in my bed, trying to take it all in. I MUST be able to see. There HAS to be a way out.

Oh, Chuck, If you were only here. I need you so.

Chapter Four

Boy, have I got the questions for that doctor today! And I'm sure he will be doing his best to answer them and reassure me that I will be able to cope. It's easy to see he's treated a lot of people in the past so he must know something about it. But, still, he has never experienced blindness himself. I know he wants to help. It's just that I don't think anyone can help. It's going to be up to me to make my own way, as always.

I guess I had better ask Mr. Whitman for a week off. Shouldn't have any problem there, and I need a little time to pull myself together. I'll just tell him I have a little physical problem and need to be relieved of the pressure for a few days.

"Of course, Angela. You should have taken some time before this. A little rest will do you a world of good. Just take care of yourself and get well soon. Come back and make a fortune for us."

"Thank you, Mr. Whitman," as I laugh wryly to myself.

Oh, yes. I'll make a fortune! I won't even be able to work. You can't make sketches and designs when you can't see the paper under your pencil. It doesn't matter what's in my head, if I can't put it on the paper, the seamstress won't be able to construct anything. Oh, if there was only some way I could transfer my thoughts to sketches. But it's impossible.

~ ~ ~ ~ ~ ~ ~ ~ ~ ~ ~ ~

On my first day at home, I'll not try to accomplish much. Just unwind. I won't even think. I'll just check over the "new" house and yard and see what I've got here. I moved in such a hurry and have been away so much, I'm not too familiar with things.

Now what did I do with those receipts for the meter deposits? They must be in this drawer -- somewhere. Oh, -- there's one of Chuck's old notebooks. As I hold it close, it is almost as if I can feel the warmth of his hands.

'Oh, Chuck! Why did you have to go? I'm so alone -- and going blind. How will I ever manage? There is just no way.' And I collapse on the floor, crying my heart out.

~ ~ ~ ~ ~ ~ ~ ~ ~ ~ ~ ~ ~

Well, being at home for a few days has served one good purpose. It has made me aware that I had better make some detailed plans about how I'm going to live in the immediate future.

Of course, it's going to take money. Where's that last bank statement? Let's see how I stand. Looks like a lot of the money I got from the sale of our big house has gone to buy this one. But there's some left, and with Chuck's insurance I should be able to get by for a while until I can come up with a way to earn a living. I'm sure glad I found this smaller place. Since I'm not loaded with cash, I won't be able to hire much help -- maybe a cleaning lady a couple of days a month. So I'm going to have to learn to manage on my own.

I'll just -- Oh, I can't do anything if I can't see. All my beautiful plans -- crushed. It's so unfair. I've never done anything to deserve all this. Where's Daddy's God now? If He would just materialize, I would like to have a talk with Him. I'd ask Him why He's picking on me. I'm not a bad person. None of this is my fault. If there is a God, it's His fault. (Oh, maybe I shouldn't have thought that. He'll probably hold it against me.) But I'm so frustrated, so confused, so miserable. And so ALONE. So very alone!

Maybe I ought to call Dad. But what could he do? He would just be more upset and rush up here to "help" me. No, I'm probably a lot better off on my own without all his reminders about God.

~ ~ ~ ~ ~ ~ ~ ~ ~ ~ ~ ~ ~

When I come back to work, I am determined to do my very best as long as I can. But I keep making stupid mistakes because I can't see clearly. Now Mr. Whitman has called me in to talk about my sloppy work.

Can't say as I blame him. But what can I do? Except apologize and promise to be extra careful in the future. But I find I can't look at him as I make this foolish promise.

Mr. Whitman has stopped talking, and is reaching for my hands. Now he's speaking more quietly. "Angela, what's wrong? Somehow I get the feeling that there is more here than meets the eye."

I try to laugh, but it sounds more like a sob. "Oh, Mr. Whitman, I didn't want to tell you – at least, not yet. I had hoped it wouldn't happen so quickly. I have so many ideas, so many plans. I'm still trying to work my way through my grief. But I guess you have to know some time. Mr. Whitman, I am going blind and nothing can be done." Then I begin to cry in spite of myself.

I've always been a very calm, composed person. I've certainly never cried in public, even after Chuck's death. Mr. Whitman didn't seem to know what to make of it. He got out his handkerchief and put his arm around me.

Finally I calmed down a little, so I apologized for my lack of control.

"Look, my Dear," he said, "It appears that you may have reason to be out of control. If this is as bad as you say, I don't see how you have kept going this long. Is there anything that can be done?"

"I'm afraid not, Sir. I have the help of one of the best doctors in this part of the country, and he gives me no hope. He just seems to think I'll learn to handle it. He certainly has a lot more confidence in me than I have."

"What are you plans? It is evident that you will not be able to continue like this much longer."

"I guess I really haven't thought it through. Just planned to keep going as long as I could. But it looks like I'm almost at the end of that line. I'll get my work in order so someone else can take over and then I'll report back to you at the end of the week."

~ ~ ~ ~ ~ ~ ~ ~ ~ ~ ~ ~

It seems that all my projects are in order as far as I can take them. I've discussed some of the details with Mary Jane, my assistant. The only thing left to do is to get back to Mr. Whitman.

Looks like he's been waiting for me. After I sit down, his secretary brings in coffee, then leaves us alone.

It's hard for Mr. Whitman to get started. I wish I could help him. But I don't know what to say either.

Finally, he speaks. "Angela, you have done so much for this firm over the past few years. You are one of the most efficient and creative people we ever had. I find -- a -- It's so hard to say, good-bye."

"Be sure to stop by Personnel before you check out. When we contracted for disability insurance for our employees I certainly never expected a time like this. But how thankful I am that we did. I'm not sure how much your benefits will be, but they should help you over the rough places. Of course, the Company will continue to pay your regular salary for the first three months you are off. Then the insurance will take over. Miss Prim will need you to complete some forms. Also she will help you check with the Social Security people. I'm sure there will be some compensation there. Oh, Angela -- Oh, if there were only something I could do. I feel so helpless."

"Thank you, Mr. Whitman. You are being more than kind. I had no idea I would be eligible for any income once I quit working. You don't know what this will mean to me. Surely I will find some means of livelihood in time. But right now, I just can't think. It will really be a blessing not to have to worry about money for a while."

"Well, if there is nothing else, perhaps I had better go to the Personnel Department and then clean out my desk. As you might expect, I haven't mentioned my problem to the others. They are very kind people and I just couldn't take their pity right now. After I'm gone, if anyone should ask, I don't mind your telling them the reason for my leaving. I would hate for them to think I had been fired."

"No one could ever think that, My Dear. Do take care of yourself. When you are feeling better, stop by, and visit. I should like to keep in touch. You have made a real contribution to this Company, young lady, and that won't be forgotten."

"Thank you, again." I put out my hand and Mr. Whitman clasped it in both of his. Then he turned abruptly and looked out the window.

I reach for a tissue, pick up my purse and head for Personnel.

Miss Prim was expecting me and she had all the forms laid out for me to complete. Then she turned her back, pretending to put a file in the case, and began to speak in her little, quiet, far-away voice that matched her name. "Mrs. Graham, we'll miss you around here."

That's just the sort of thing I had wanted to avoid. But I couldn't doubt Miss Prim's sincerity. Impulsively I hug her, and dash out of the office.

All the other workers have called it a day and gone home. So I'll have the office all to myself. Now, I can go through things, get the rest of my stuff, and put the place in order for the next occupant. 'THE NEXT OCCUPANT' -- I wonder who he or she will be. Well, I don't have time to deal with that. I'd better get out of here. Leaving a place for the last time, a place where you've been happy, isn't easy.

~ ~ ~ ~ ~ ~ ~ ~ ~ ~ ~ ~

My, there's a lot of traffic at this hour. I'd better keep my wits about me and be extra careful. Funny how I've always been able to see three ways at once, and now, I'm not even sure what some things are when I see them.

Oh, driving is no real problem -- yet. But how am I going to get around this city when I can no longer see where I am going?

I guess some people could depend on family and neighbors. But I don't want to bother my family with this. I haven't been too bothered with them the last few years, so why should they help me now? And I don't even know any neighbors.

Seems like I always come back to the same old place. I've got no one to depend on but myself. Right now I don't see -- hmm, good pun -- how I can handle it. But there's got to be a way, if I can just find it.

Chapter Five

So here I am with what is widely known as "the first day of the rest of my life." That old cliché is pretty time-worn, but I guess it is appropriate today. And what have I done with this "first" day? Nothing.

I've been standing here among the day lilies for a good ten minutes. But they are so beautiful! And soon I won't be able to see them. As I glance around me, I see a modest, but attractive house, set back on the spacious lot with a well-kept lawn and a number of shrubs and trees. There are a few flower beds, here and there. It certainly is a pretty picture, pleasant and reassuring. It's a good place to live.

But how will I ever take care of the yard? Oh, I suppose that boy down the street will keep mowing the grass, but the flowers will need attention. Flowers were one of the things that attracted me to this place when I bought it. I've always enjoyed the little chores of digging, weeding, and watering. It's been my little concession to nature. Must I give that up, too?

As I turn away, my tears blind me and I stumble and almost fall onto the wrought iron settee. I sit there with my head in my hands. The tears come again.

Now, this will never do. There has been ample rainfall this year without my watering the grass with my tears. I feel a smile on my lips. I know that's the first time I've smiled today. There, I feel much better.

~ ~ ~ ~ ~ ~ ~ ~ ~ ~ ~ ~ ~

It's in the house and to my desk for me. One has to start somewhere. I'll hook up the old typewriter and make a list of "Essential Matters."

Let's see. Where to start? Well, one has to eat, have clean clothing, and keep the house in reasonable order. Oh, yes! 'Food, clothing, and shelter.' Somewhere in the dim, distant past, I was taught these are the essentials of life.

But that will be only existence, not life. Is that what I must settle for? What about those other "necessary" ingredients -- someone to love, something worthwhile to do, and something to look forward to? Ha! The love of my life is gone. I can't see to do my work. And there's nothing to look forward to but loneliness, sorrow, and frustration.

In a practical frame, I must have some means of transportation. Grocery shopping will be essential. Even clothing will wear out eventually and need to be replaced. No doubt there will be trips to the doctor and dentist. How can I handle this? I had better check out public transportation.

The radio and cassette tapes can help me keep in touch with the world. But everything needs maintenance. How many things I have just taken for granted!

As long as I can see, even a little, and get around by myself, I'll be fine. But I don't even know how much time I have left. Oh, how will I ever cope?

~ ~ ~ ~ ~ ~ ~ ~ ~ ~ ~ ~ ~

Well, so much for lists. While I'm wandering around here, I suddenly notice that it's almost sundown. I don't believe I've eaten anything since morning. Guess I had better make a sandwich or open a can of soup. Got to keep the old strength up.

Let's see if I can do that with my eyes closed. It will be good practice. Oh -- no. I can't even find the refrigerator without looking.

I'll turn on the TV. Maybe that will help. Not that I care anything about the programs, but the noise will help. This house won't seem quite, so empty, so lonely.

I'm so tired. But I haven't accomplished a thing all day. I suppose I should go to bed though. But I'll probably just toss and turn.

~ ~ ~ ~ ~ ~ ~ ~ ~ ~ ~ ~ ~

I must have slept some. It's morning, anyway. But what's to get up for? Can't go to work or anything. Anyway, I don't feel very well. There's a queasy sensation in the pit of my stomach. I'll doze if I can.

Nine o'clock! I can't stand this bed any longer. A fresh cup of coffee will help.

As I sit here and look around the kitchen, one thing is very clear. If I am to live alone, and be unable to see, I must know exactly where things are. Although I've lived here almost a month, I still haven't put things in order as I should. So I'll start with the cabinets.

Hey, this is kind of fun. It feels good to accomplish something worthwhile some- time. I could sit around here and mope forever. But all this work needs to be done, and the time passes more quickly when you are busy.

Looks like I'll have time for a quick walk around the block before bed time.

~ ~ ~ ~ ~ ~ ~ ~ ~ ~ ~ ~

At least I slept better last night. I think I had a bad dream toward morning, though. I can't quite remember it. But it was sad.

Uh-oh. What's wrong with this silly stomach? Maybe a cup of coffee would help.

~ ~ ~ ~ ~ ~ ~ ~ ~ ~ ~ ~

In the last few days I've been able to get the house in order and work out a system for my housework. I'm thankful for my good memory. I must try to remember where things are.

Perhaps I should do some things blindfolded as I work about the place. It will help me get the feel of things. But it's so hard! I keep wanting to peek. Oh, I can't do anything like this. I may as well give up. Now, look, Old Girl. That attitude won't get it. Put that blindfold back on and try again.

The door bell? Who could that be? I don't know anyone around here. Actually I really don't want to know them. Blindness is a do-it-yourself project and I don't have the time to get involved with people. Oh, well. Guess I had better answer it.

"Hello."

"Hello to you." She is a cute little brunette, about five feet, two, with a happy smile on her face and a covered dish in her hand.

"I'm Becky Rogers from across the street. I'm ashamed I've waited so long to welcome you to the block. But at first, I thought you worked and I didn't know when a convenient time would be. Then when I realized you were home, I just kept putting it off. But I'll really do better in the future, if you'll forgive me."

She catches me off guard, so I mumble, "Oh, that's all right. Please come in."

I take her into the living room and she thrusts her offering of walnut brownies into my hand. "I wasn't sure how many were in your family and if you had any children. My kids think they can't live all week without, at least, one batch of brownies."

"Uh -- no. I don't have any children. I'm a widow. There's only me." I didn't mean to let her see my pain, but I couldn't help it.

"Oh, I'm so sorry." Becky looks confused and turns her eyes away. Then she says, "Oh, well, you can eat them yourself until you are sick of them. Then give them to the cat or the birds." She gives a nervous little laugh.

"Thank you. It was very kind of you. I'm sorry the house is in such a mess. I just lost my husband a few weeks ago. That's why I sold our old home and moved here. So I really don't have everything in order yet. Please --"

"Oh, think nothing of it. Anyway, it looks great to me. We've lived in our house for five years, and it is still a mess. But with two little ones, I never seem to get around to everything."

"Yes, well --." But I couldn't think of anything to say.

"Sorry. I won't keep you. I know you are busy. I just wanted to say, 'hello.' Besides I had better get back and see what my little Indians are up to. It's good to have such a pretty young lady for a neighbor. I just know we're going to be great friends."

This is kind of embarrassing. I realized I had not been very gracious to her, and she seemed so nice. But I'm just not up to neighborliness right now.

"Thank you for coming. I'll return your bowl in a few days."

As Becky leaves, I think, 'Where was I in this blindness business?' Oh, yes, I was trying to dust this shelf without looking, and without breaking anything. Crash!! -- there goes the little rose vase. Oh, what's the use? Why don't I just give up? I'll never be able to do things right.

I drop into a chair and stare off into space. It's all so hopeless.

Chapter Six

When I woke up this morning, I was determined to jump right out of bed and get things done. All of this taking it easy and feeling sorry for myself isn't good. But the minute I put a foot on the floor, the room began to go round and round. I made it to the bathroom before I threw up. I had to go back to bed for a while.

Finally, I tried again, but I felt pretty queasy. Must have been something I ate. Becky's brownies? Oh, no! I forgot to try them, so it couldn't have been them. A cup of coffee helped, and I forgot about it as the day wore on.

After going to the bank to arrange some of my affairs, and doing some shopping, I got my hair done. That did me a world of good. I feel almost human again.

Another morning and another upset stomach. I don't understand it. Maybe it is the forty-eight hour "bug." But a light breakfast seems to help

There's still a lot to be done around here, but day by day, I'm getting things in shape. I haven't figured out a way to ward off these spells of grief that stab me at the most unexpected times. Or the depression. I really thought I was stronger than this. This upset stomach every morning is really getting to me. Sometimes coffee helps. Sometimes it doesn't. Sometimes just the smell of food sends me rushing to the bathroom.

The only thing I can figure out is that I've got a bad case of "nerves." This is probably what is called, "a nervous stomach." After all, I've been through a lot lately, with Chuck's death, moving, giving up my position, and learning that I'm going blind. This is enough to throw a nervous system completely out of line.

But just deciding what's wrong with me doesn't correct the problem. I don't know what to do for it. Making emotional adjustments take time. I suppose the reasonable thing to do is to see a physician. But I don't want to. I never did like going to the doctor. And he'll want to probe my emotional distress to find a related cause. I just don't feel like sharing my deepest thoughts and feelings with a stranger.

After a couple of weeks of this, it looks like I have no other choice. Since I don't know a physician, I'll just have to look in the phone directory for a name. Let's see -- 'Physicians and Surgeons -- Medical -- MD -- Psychiatry -- Dr. Paul Sandler.' As good as any, I guess. I'll call for an appointment.

In Dr. Sandler's office, I completed the required questionnaire. Then the nurse ushered me into the doctor's office, where she asked me to disrobe and put on one of those "lovely" hospital gowns.

She took my temperature, blood pressure and weighed me. All I can do now is sit and wait for the doctor. What will he tell me? Surely this isn't something serious. After all, how much can one person take?

Out of the past, comes this little saying, "God will not put upon us more than we can bear." I don't put much confidence in that. If God does exist, He has long since forgotten about me.

Suddenly, I look up, and there's a smiling Doctor Sandler.

"Good morning." He looks at the chart. "You're Mrs. Graham?"

"Yes."

I try to answer his smile with one of my own, but it doesn't come off very well.

"I see you have some physical problems that might be emotionally related. Tell me about them. What made you think you may have emotional problems?"

"Doctor, I --" Then I burst into tears. I couldn't help it. It was so embarrassing. "Oh, I'm so sorry. I don't usually act like this."

"That's quite all right. I understand. Mrs. Graham, I've been in his business a long time, so nothing you can say will upset me in the least. Please feel free to begin at the beginning and tell me what's troubling you. Just pretend you are talking to your Father."

That did it. I was off into the tears again. Why did he have to mention Dad? Oh, if only I could talk to him. He's always stood by me whenever I gave him the chance. Now this doctor mention of him reminds me I've been ungrateful, maybe even unfair to him.

Dr. Sandler waited quietly until I was able to calm down a little. He handed me a tissue. "It seems we've gotten off to a 'good' start. I must have said something that upset you and I'm sorry."

"No, Doctor. It's my fault. And I am the one who is sorry. Sorry for so many things. You mentioned my father, and I was suddenly overcome with the realization that I haven't discussed this with him, or much of anything else in my life for a long time. I have a wonderful father, but I've been inclined to forget that. Now, I'll try to do better." I sit straighter in my chair and try to smile.

"My immediate, problem, Doctor, is my stomach. It seems to be upset all the time. I throw up a lot. And I don't know what's causing it. I don't know what to do about it. It is very uncomfortable and it is irritating -- I have too much to do right now. But this discomfort keeps slowing me down. It is very frustrating."

"The reason that I thought it might have some connection with my emotional state, is that I've had some very upsetting things in my life lately and I just assumed they may be expressing themselves in this problem. Does that sound reasonable to you?"

"Well, yes. That might very well be the case. But we cannot rule out possible physical causes without an examination, perhaps certain tests. Before we begin, do you feel like telling me about these 'upsetting' things?"

"Of course. First, Doctor, my husband was killed in a tragic traffic accident a short time ago, and my whole world fell apart. We were very much in love, quite successful in our work and our lives were well-ordered. Then abut three weeks ago, I was told that I am going blind, and I have been forced to give up my position as a fashion designer." That was about all I could manage without crying again. I looked at my hands in my lap.

"Oh, you poor child. I think I can understand something of your feelings. And you are so young to have to face these great tragedies. Mrs. Graham, as you know, besides being a medical doctor I am a psychiatrist. You understand the meaning of the term or you would not have come to me. But there is something I must say. I have had extensive training and a number of years of experience, but there is just so much a human being can do. I remind you, as I do all my patients, that while I am limited, we have a Great Physician who has no such limitations. I will do what I can for you, but your faith will mean much more toward your healing than anything I can do. Do you understand?"

"Yes, Doctor. I suppose so. But I must tell you that I'm not sure I believe in God any more, at least not a personal God who cares about us and cares for us. My Mother died of cancer just when I needed her most. At that time, I realized God turned his back on me. I'm not sure why. Up until that time, I had attended church all my life, even made a profession of faith and joined the church. But that made no difference to Him. So I have gone my own way in the years since then. If, as you seem to believe, He cares, why does He keep punishing me by taking my husband and my sight? If I get through this, it will be with your help and my own will power. God has nothing for me." I know I sounded bitter.

The doctor looked at me intently and shook his head. Finally he spoke. "Perhaps the best thing for us to do is to begin the examination and see where we go from there. Will you please seat yourself on the table, lie back and relax."

Dr. Sandler made a careful examination in all areas, and when he completed the internal phase, he smiled, extended his hand to me and lifted me into a sitting position.

"Well, Mrs. Graham. Well, well. I'm happy to disprove your recently expressed and carefully thought out idea of God's neglect of you. I have some great news for you. I do not think you have emotional problems. Oh, I'm not discounting your emotional and mental distress over your recent loses. And, if you like, I shall be glad to counsel with you a few sessions. But I believe your physical problem will soon take care of itself. You do not have some rare disease or tragic malfunction of your internal organs. Mrs. Graham, you are pregnant!"

"Don't you see, God does provide for His children. Oh, He allows the ills of the world to touch our lives at times, but it isn't His will that we suffer. He really cares for us. In this case, He has provided just what you need. I suppose, if you get right down to it, that's what He does for each of us."

"Pregnant? Doctor, what are you talking about? I just told you my husband was killed a short time ago. This is ridiculous!" The Doctor was making me angry.

"Yes, I know you did. But this baby should arrive in a little less than six months. Count back and see if I'm not right. At any rate, you're definitely pregnant. You should be very happy. Now you have a part of that loving husband and an expression of your love for each other."

"Oh, Doctor. I know you are a fine man and believe every word that you have been saying. I wish I had your faith. But I don't. And I certainly don't see how being pregnant is going to solve anything. Doctor, I'm going blind! How can I possibly take care of a baby, to say nothing of rearing the child? I'm not even able to work and make a living. Oh, this is terrible!"

He patted me on the back. "There, there. I can see this is a bit of a shock. May take a little getting used to. But it will work out. You'll see. Now, get dressed and when I come back, I will give you the name of an excellent obstetrician. My nurse will make your first appointment." He closed the door quietly.

As I dress, my thoughts go round and round. I'm more confused than ever. Whatever shall I do?

Chapter Seven

Somehow I found my way out of the doctor's office and located my car in the parking area. After unlocking the door, I slid in and just sat under the wheel. My mind was in a turmoil and I could find no point of reason in the whole mess. It seems so unreal. Surely there was some mistake. All these things can't be happening to me. One day, life was perfect with a handsome husband and the Fashion World at my feet. Then a couple of months later, I'm a widow, expecting a child, and facing blindness. Impossible! No one person could handle all this. It just isn't right. It's a nightmare. Surely I'll wake up soon.

No, it's real all right. It is happening to me. I HAVE to face it. But how can I? I'm so alone. There's no one to whom I can turn for help. I have no close friends and my family is all far away. But I don't want to ask them for help. I didn't have any trouble convincing them that I could handle Chuck's death because I've always been self-reliant and independent. I've never needed anything from any of them and I don't have time to become involved in their lives. There is no one!

I don't remember starting the car or driving home. But I must have, because as I turned into the driveway, I saw a small boy. He would ultimately change the course of my life. He must have been about seven years old, running full speed ahead, across my yard, as I pulled the car to a stop.

The brilliant sunshine of an early May morning made his red curls look as if the were burning like fire. His numerous freckles gave an expression of mischief to the wide grin that covered his face.

Just before he reached the driveway, he seemed to hesitate, almost stop. A fleeting expression of fear, or uncertainty crossed his face.

I kill the engine, and roll down the window. "Hi," I call.

"Hi," he answered. And the grin returned. "You're Mrs. Graham, aren't you? My Mom told me how pretty you are and that you don't have any little boys. So I wanted to come and ask you to go with us to the Bible School Commencement at our church. You will, won't you? You will have fun. There is going to be a program and everything. And you can see the bird house I made. You'll come, won't you?" And he paused for breath.

I had to smile in spite of myself. "My, that was quite a speech. And a speedy one, too, I might add. And you forgot to tell me your name."

He drew himself up to his full height and said, "I am William Edward Rogers, III." Then he relaxed and grinned again. "Really I'm just plain Willie. That other is what the teacher put on my report card."

"I'm happy to meet you, William Edward Rogers, III. What do you say if we go into the house and see if we can find a glass of lemonade and a cookie?"

The invitation met with another grin and a quick nod of the red head.

Inside, I set Willie at the kitchen table, pour the lemonade and put a plate of cookies in front of him. Then I sit across the table and smile. Suddenly I feel more relaxed than I have in several days.

Willie keeps going back to the subject of Bible School and keeps up a steady stream of chatter about the things he's been learning and the good times he's had.

"It's not really like school, you know. We do learn a lot of memory verses and stuff. But we have a lot of fun too, and don't have any homework. Did you ever go to Bible School when you were a kid?"

"Well, yes, as a matter of fact, I did. Many years after I got too old to go to class, I helped the teachers. My Mother played the piano. Yes, -- I went to Bible School" -- and my tired mind remembered.

"Then will you go with us? It's tomorrow night at 7 o'clock. You can ride with us so we can show you the way. Mom said we should try to leave about six-thirty. Will that be all right with you?"

"Oh, I don't know, Willie. It's good of you to ask me. But when I went to Bible School -- that was a long time ago. I don't expect I'd fit in very well now. I haven't been to church in a very long time."

"I was afraid of that. And I guess that is the main reason I wanted you to go." Willie pauses, looking down at his hands. "Our teacher told us we should love our neighbors, and when my Mom told me you didn't have any family, I knew you were the neighbor God wanted me to love." He sat perfectly still, just staring at his hands.

"Oh, Willie!" I couldn't help it. I reached out and touched his shoulder and tears came into my eyes. "I'll be pleased to go." Only the most hard-hearted person could turn down an invitation like that.

The happy grin quickly appeared. Willie jumped to his feet. "Okay. See you tomorrow night then. We'll come over and pick you up." And he was gone as quickly as he had appeared.

I shake my head as I think, 'What have I done? I can't go to a Vacation Bible School Commencement. I don't even want to go. Why did I agree to?'

~ ~ ~ ~ ~ ~ ~ ~ ~ ~ ~ ~ ~

But here I am at Willie's Commencement. And I have to admit that the program is pretty good. Of course, it's just a group of small children reciting Bible verses and singing choruses, but they know their stuff. The people are so warm and friendly. They made me almost glad I came.

But I could have made it just fine without that little speech from the Pastor. All of this takes me back to a time, so long ago -- Mother was there. I was happy. Secure. Certainly a far cry from where I am today. Oh, why did I come? I knew better. I don't belong here.

Now, here's Willie to take me to view his handiwork, the great and wonderful bird house. It's a pretty good bird house, especially for a small boy. When I tell him, I'm rewarded with one of his famous grins.

Soon we are back at my house. As I get out of their car, I thank the Rogers' for the evening and the transportation. They, in turn, tell me how glad they are that I was able to go. They will see me soon.

Safely inside my own door, I kick off my shoes and collapse on the couch. My body and mind are numb. I just sit there, almost without thinking. Then I notice the ticking of the clock and realize it's past bed time. I'm so tired most of the time any more. It can't be because I work so hard because I hardly accomplish anything.

In bed, my eyes stare into the darkness. Sleep won't come. Scenes from the VBS Commencement keep going over and over in my mind. I feel so uncomfortable – even guilty. Now why should I feel guilty? I haven't done anything wrong. Except, of course, to be hit by tragedy on every hand. Maybe just being in the unfamiliar atmosphere of a church is disturbing.

Surely, in the morning I will feel better. -- Then I drift off to sleep.

Chapter Eight

Right on schedule, as soon as I woke up this morning, I experienced my usual "morning sickness." I should be getting used to it by now, but instead, it gets worse. Along with it, I have these "weepy" sessions. Can't seem to help it.

Maybe the morning coffee will help. But as I sit here and drink it, and try to pull myself and my thoughts together, I just stare out of the window. I'm not getting anywhere. I may as well admit it. This is just one of those days when I'll do well to put one foot in front of the other.

The phone startles me. Who could be calling me? A crisp, polite voice questions, "Mrs. Graham?"

"Yes,--"

"This is Nurse Snider in Dr. Sandler's office. The Doctor asked me to make an appointment for you with Dr. Michael Kradel, an obstetrician. Dr. Kradel's office is in the Medical Building at Grand and Twenty-first Street. Your appointment is for ten o'clock on Wednesday, the twenty-fifth. Will that be satisfactory, Mrs. Graham?"

"Yes, I suppose so. Wait, let me get my pen and write this down. Please give me that address and time again."

I make notes and thank the nurse.

A look at the calendar tells me that the twenty-fifth is two weeks from tomorrow. How I dread this appointment. Wish I could put it off, or just forget it altogether. Oh, that is so childish. Maybe Dr. Sandler was mistaken. But that's not likely. I'll just have to go and get it over with. At least I should learn what's expected of me so I can begin to make preparations. If this is something that has to be done, then I must do it.

In the meantime, there is definitely plenty of work around here to keep me busy. That old plan of practicing a chore until one can do it blindfolded, certainly applies to me. There are countless other blind people in this city. If they can manage, so can I.

But the big question is "How?" I can still see pretty well, yet there are many things I cannot do, even now -- thread a needle, see the line on the measuring cup, or tell time by the clock across the room. I'm almost afraid to drive in traffic. But I must continue that as long as I can. I'll just have to be extra careful.

~ ~ ~ ~ ~ ~ ~ ~ ~ ~ ~ ~ ~ ~

At last, the two weeks have passed and this is the day of my appointment with the obstetrician. I feel no better about it now than I did two weeks ago. But, at least, I won't have to dread it any longer.

Finding the Medical Building was no problem. I didn't have to wait long before being shown into the examining room. After completing the form on my medical history, the nurse had me undress and prepare for the examination.

Dr. Michael Kradel is a pleasant young man, only a few years older than me. I like his efficient, business-like manner, and his calm and kind assessment of my condition.

"Mrs. Graham, at this point, I can only confirm Dr. Sandler's judgment. I believe you to be about three months pregnant. In checking your medical history, I would calculate your due date to be the twenty-fifth of November. I also notice that you have mentioned no health problems of any consequence, so we shall expect you to have a routine pregnancy."

"Just a minute, Doctor Kradel. I realize you haven't had time to study the forms thoroughly, but I did mention one serious health problem -- my imminent blindness. I see no way I can care for a baby when I become blind."

"Of course, I was referring to any diseases or physical problems connected with the pregnancy. Your general health is good. Your measurements are adequate. If you follow instructions about diet, weight control, and exercise, all should go well. I'm not equipped to advise you about your blindness. I'm sure it is very frightening at this point. But let me try to reassure you. Others in your position, my own Mother among them, have managed quite well, and I feel confident of your ability to do the same. I will not tell you it will be easy, but I believe it will work out in time."

Handing me prescriptions for calcium and vitamins and saying that he wants to see me again in a month, the doctor bids me a pleasant, "Good day," and leaves.

I wish I had the confidence that these doctors seem to have in me. It's easy for them to say because they don't have to do it. No one really seems to understand.

~ ~ ~ ~ ~ ~ ~ ~ ~ ~ ~ ~

As I walk in the door at home, the phone is ringing. It's my neighbor, Becky Rogers.

"Hi, Angela. A group of us women from the church are getting together at my house tomorrow afternoon to work on our Food Pantry and Clothes Closet projects. Since you haven't had a chance to meet many people yet, we would like for you to join us and get acquainted. They are a fun group and we're involved in some practical stuff."

"Oh, I don't know, Becky. I haven't been feeling very well lately. In fact, I have just come from the doctor's office."

"Hey, I hope there's nothing seriously wrong. Hang on. I'll be over in just a few minutes."

And before I could stop her, she hung up. I see her walking up the drive way. Why can't I keep my mouth shut? I've managed this far without involving others. There's no need for the whole neighborhood to learn of my troubles.

"Come in, Becky. I'm sorry I startled you. It's nothing serious, I'm sure. You know how we women are -- all our little aches and pains."

"Now, look, Angela -- I realize we don't know each other very well. You may think I'm just some old busybody prying into a neighbor's business. If you want me to leave, I will. But this is not a case of idle curiosity. I sensed the first day we met that there is something very serious troubling you. Maybe it would help to talk about it. If you don't want me to talk about it with anyone else, I will keep your confidence. But sometimes, it helps to share our burdens."

Becky is such a kind person and I can tell by the earnest expression on her face that she meant well. It would be so good to have someone to talk to. I have been so isolated. But then, I would have to admit my weakness and fears. And that's hard.

"Becky, I know you are concerned. And you are such a good neighbor. It's just that, - - Oh, Becky, I'm so alone. I just can't handle all this - -." As

I spread my hands in a defeated gesture, the tears suddenly, unexpectedly stream down my face. I am so embarrassed. I grope vainly for a tissue. Becky hands me one from her jacket pocket and puts her warm, gentle arms around me. We sit on the couch, with no one saying a word for a minute until I begin to get myself under control.

"There, that's better." Becky gives me a crooked grin that immediately reminds me of a certain little, red headed, freckled-faced boy.

"Now, I know where Willie gets his grin," I say with a feeble smile. "Maybe it would help to let you know how I feel. The trouble is that I'm not exactly sure how I DO feel."

Then I began telling her about Chuck and our great life together. And how the whole world collapsed with the accident.

She responds with tears in her own eyes. "Oh, you poor girl, I don't think I could handle it if I lost my husband, Eddie. No wonder you are having a bad time. We will just have to be more supportive. They tell me these things get better with time. But I'm not so sure. But maybe time does help one to adjust."

"Well, Becky, remember you asked for this. There's more." I try to smile, but I can feel it is more like a smirk.

"I told you I have just been to see the doctor. He tells me that I am going to have a baby. It should be born about November twenty-fifth. Poor little human being, with no father." And I start crying again.

This time Becky smiles broadly through her tears. "Oh, isn't that wonderful! Chuck really isn't gone after all. Don't you see? This is God's own special blessing for you."

Suddenly I feel agitated and cold. Becky doesn't understand at all. She has no idea about being alone and facing the prospect of trying to rear a child, (a child that I never asked for) under my circumstances. She wants to say that all this is because God is so good to me.

"Ah, Becky, before you get too excited about this, maybe I had better tell you that I do not share your enthusiasm for God's goodness. Long ago, I, like you, had been taught that God loves us all and cares for us. But that was back before my Mother died just when I needed her most, before Chuck was taken from me so brutally, before I was given the responsibility of rearing a child alone, before I learned --." I caught myself just in time. I had almost told her about the blindness. I do not intend to do that. Her sermons are bad enough. I do not want her pity, too.

Becky gives me a funny expression. She puts her hand on my arm, saying, "Hey, take it easy. This has been a rough day for you. What you need now is to put your feet up and take a little nap. This has been tiring physically, as well as emotionally. I'll stop by again after supper, just to make sure you're all right."

She slips quietly out the door, and before I know it, I have drifted off to sleep.

Guess Becky was right. I was more tired than I thought. And I do feel somewhat better. I don't have to face everything today. But tomorrow, I must begin working on a system to enable me to get through what lies ahead.

When Becky stops back by, she is pleased to see me looking more human. But I'm quick to tell her that I don't think it is a good idea for me to meet with her church ladies tomorrow. Surprisingly she agrees with me and leaves soon, saying she will call me later.

Chapter Nine

It startled me to see the sun shinning through the window and the clock telling me it was seven a.m. It had been such a good time. Chuck was back and things were just as they had always been. We were so happy.

I stretched, like a sleepy kitten, and my arm fell across the other side of the bed -- the empty bed. I became fully awake. Chuck was not here. Chuck was gone. He wasn't coming back. It was all a dream. And my momentary happiness dissolved into a weeping spell of despair.

Suddenly I sit up, and with a shake of my head, give myself a stern lecture. 'Look here, Girl! This will never do. You have responsibilities, remember? In less than six months you will have a baby to care for, and at about the same time, you will be blind. So, up and at 'em! You have no time to lie in bed and cry at seven o'clock in the morning.'

Quickly I dress, make the bed and go to the kitchen for some kind of breakfast. Not that I really want anything, but good sense (which I don't seem to have a lot of lately) tells me I am to think of someone besides myself. Someone I don't even know. Someone who doesn't seem real. But someone who needs nourishment and special care. So I must try to do right by him -- her -- it. "It" should have a name. Maybe that would make it more real. Let's see -- how about --? No, maybe -- "Tater Tot?" 'That's it, you poor little half orphan. You now have a name. What shall we have for breakfast, Tater Tot?'

'I'd like a bit of orange juice, myself. And maybe some toast and jelly. But that's probably not enough for you. Maybe we should have some cereal. Yeah, I think that is a good idea.'

Hope no one hears me talking to myself. They will think I'm really 'over the hill.' Maybe I am, for all I know. I'm not making a lot of sense right now. On the other hand, talking to my baby makes pretty good sense. Helps me to realize I'm not really alone any more.

About the middle of the morning, Becky calls to check on me. I tell her I'm doing fine, trying to adjust to the shock. Then I think to ask about the ladies' church work, and she reports they are having fun and doing a lot of good things.

Just before we hang up, she says, "Oh, by the way, are you going to be free to go shopping with me on Thursday?"

This is certainly a surprise, but I can think of no reason not to go. So, I say, "Sure. What time are you planning on going?"

"Oh, ten o'clock or there about. My kids are spending the day with their cousins about four blocks from here, so when I get them delivered and settled, we'll have the rest of the day for ourselves. I'll take our car, if you don't mind, because I know where everything is around here."

That sounded good to me. I wouldn't have to face the traffic. "Wonderful," I say. "I'll buy lunch."

"Great. See you then." Becky hangs up. And I sit down to think about it.

It's been a long time since I've been shopping. And it has always been a "hurry-up" job. Get what I had to have, and go. I'm looking forward to seeing how Becky handles shopping. Should be interesting.

As I prepare to go about my work the next two days, I try to think of things I should look for while I'm out. I start a list. A pair of hose is the first item. And tooth paste. I'm petty well stocked with groceries, though, perhaps I should get a bottle of milk.

~ ~ ~ ~ ~ ~ ~ ~ ~ ~ ~ ~

I'm trying to plan for the future, but it is such strange territory, I hardly know how to plan. I guess the nursery will have to be located in that smaller room across from my bedroom. Maybe that's something I should shop for. It will need some furniture. Becky will have good ideas.

As I began to rearrange some things in my room, I come across Mom's old Bible. It's pretty well worn, but I've saved it all these years because it was hers.

Oh -- here in the middle is the "Family Page," with all the children listed and their birthdays. And also when they were saved and baptized.

I didn't know she had recorded those. I must save this for Tater Tot. Oh, I wish Mother were here now. She would help me with all this. I still don't understand why she had to go. Here I am, crying again. I'm doing just too much of this lately. Must be my hormones acting up.

Time to think about food again. That's one thing the doctor stresses -- regular, nourishing meals.

Another day is almost gone, with very little to show for it. I'm going to have to learn to "speed it up."

Chapter Ten

There's Becky turning into the driveway. I guess I have everything -- my walking shoes and my purse. So here we go --.

Becky is a careful driver, and she seems to know where she is going. Oh, here is West Center Village. I've been by here, but have never stopped.

As we park, Becky turns to me. "Well, what's the first item on your list?" she asks.

"I -- a -- guess some hose," I stammer.

"Oh," she said, "We're going to do some serious shopping. How about some maternity clothes?"

Wow! I hadn't even thought of that. Soon I won't be able to wear my regular clothes, so I guess she has the right idea.

Becky adds, "but we'll not go overboard today. You don't need a lot yet. Let's look for some 'knock-about' stuff -- pants that stretch around the tummy, and a few loose tops. Maybe one nice dress for Sunday or going out. How does that sound?"

"Sounds pretty reasonable to me. I just never thought -- Oh, this is all so new. I don't really know what I'm doing."

"Ah, let me be your guide. I've done this twice, you know, so I'm an 'expert.' Let's visit the 'Stork Shop.'"

Inside we see a large display of maternity clothes. I've designed a lot of things, but nothing like this. Should be interesting from a professional view point.

"Here are some cute tops. I would suggest you get three for now. You can always add more later, if you need them. Do you sew? Tops are easy to make."

"No, I really don't sew. I guess I've never mentioned my professional work to you, have I? I am, or was, a fashion designer. But not maternity clothes."

Becky stares at me -- "Wait a minute. Angela Graham -- of course! There are a couple of fancy dress shops uptown that have your name all over the place. I've never been inside, but have drooled over the models in the windows. I just never made the connection. Here I am trying to tell you about buying clothes. That's a good laugh, isn't it?"

"Now, Becky, I've never bought this type of clothing before. Even though I was a designer, I need all the help I can get."

"What do you mean, you *were* a designer?"

"That's how I made my living for several years."

"Why did you stop? I can imagine it was a pretty good living."

"Ah -- Becky. Could we talk about this some other time? Let's shop while we have the chance."

Becky gives me a strange look, but turns back to the clothes on the rack.

We soon find a few attractive tops and some baggy pants and we start looking for the dress section. I find myself thinking I could design something much better than these. Of course, that would be if I could see. I finally select a navy blue with white trim. Not too bad. It will do for now, or quite a while, I hope. I'm really not showing much yet.

We stop for lunch at a cute little Tea Room, and enjoy an elegant chicken salad sandwich with our tea, and a lot of giggling and laughing like a couple of school girls. I don't know when I've felt so good, so relaxed.

As we finish eating, Becky says, "You know what -- 'Who's it' is going to need a nursery."

"Hey, just a minute. 'Who's it' has a name already."

"Yeah? What is it?"

"Tater Tot."

"Tater Tot?" Becky giggles. " That's great! I love tater tots. That's a wonderful name selection."

"Well, I'm glad you approve. I've thought about using the smaller room across from my bed room for a nursery. But it is going to need some work."

"Naturally. I'll come over tomorrow and we'll make some plans. Need to check out the space. Is it empty now?"

"Well, no, not exactly. I've put some stuff in there. I didn't know what else to do with it. There's not a lot. I can put some of the boxes in the attic and spread the other things in a different room."

"Okay, but don't you go climbing up to the attic. Eddie will come over after work this evening and put the boxes away for you."

"I would appreciate that, but I hate to bother him."

"No bother. When you know him better, you will see that helping people is what makes him happy."

So we make plans for the next morning, then stop by the grocery store for a few things and head home, stopping briefly to pick up Willie and his little sister, Jean. They look a little grimy, but have happy smiles on their faces as they wave good-bye to their cousins.

I didn't realize I was so tired until I gathered my packages and climbed out of Becky's car. I thanked her again for a good day, and she drove across the street to her house.

It felt almost impossible to climb the front steps into the house. After dropping the bundles on the couch, I stepped out of my shoes, and collapsed in the recliner.

~ ~ ~ ~ ~ ~ ~ ~ ~ ~ ~ ~ ~

I guess I must have dozed off, for when I next looked around, it was getting dark. I struggled to my feet and went in search of some quick nourishment. I found a can of vegetable soup and some crackers.

I finish the food, clean the kitchen and start bed preparations. First, of course, I must hang up my purchases.

The telephone? At this hour? I guess Becky thought of something else.

"Hello."

"Angela --?"

"Doris? Doris, what's wrong?"

"Oh, Angela. It's Dad. We've just taken him to the emergency room. I thought you might want to know."

"*Might* want to know? Of course, I want to know. -- Oh, I'm sorry. I hope you can understand why I said that, but I do love Dad. Tell me what happened."

" Well, he's not been feeling well. He has been in pain for three days, but like one of his stubborn daughters, he didn't tell anyone."

"*One* of his stubborn daughters. You mean he has more than one?"

"Oh, Angela, be serious. Today, his problem became so painful he finally had to ask for help. We rushed him to the hospital as quickly as possible, but we've had a very long wait in the ER before they could examine him. So no one has told us anything yet."

"All right. I'll get there as soon as I can. I haven't been feeling up to par lately, and this has been a tiring day. But I'll come the first thing in the morning. Which hospital is he in?"

"Community General."

"Okay. If you can give me the phone number there in the waiting room, I'll get back to you as soon as I check the bus schedule."

"Just a minute. Let me check the phone. The area code is 816 -- 928-5566. Got it?"

"Got it. I'll call you right back."

Then I dial the bus station and call Doris back with the information that the bus for Maplesville leaves at eight a.m. and should get there around eleven-thirty or a little after. I will take a cab to the hospital.

"Okay, then. Be careful," she cautions.

"Sure. You, too. - - Love you, Doris."

And I hang up quickly, so I won't have to explain why I needed to say that. Maybe I don't need my family, but maybe they need me. It could be that I need them, too. I don't know why Dad's illness has shaken me up so.

Guess I had better call Becky and let her know what's going on. She'll keep an eye on things for me. I'll leave the house key in the mail box so she can find it.

Now a quick shower and to bed. Tomorrow will be hard.

Chapter Eleven

It was a tiring ride. We had one stop-over, and I got out and walked a bit. That helped.

We pulled into the Maplesville Bus Station at eleven-fifteen and as quickly as I could get a taxi, I was on my way to the hospital.

I inquired at the desk about Russell Dobson and was told that he was in Room 214. Yes, he was allowed to have visitors. So I rushed to the elevator.

I quietly opened the door and looked in. Dad appeared to be asleep. Doris was sitting in a chair nearby, staring out the window.

As I closed the door behind me, she looked up with a startled expression on her face, appearing uncertain about how to react.

I set my bag on the floor, put my purse on the foot of the bed, and held out my arms. Doris fell into my arms and put hers around me, holding on for dear life.

"Oh, Angela," she said, "I'm thankful you are here." There were tears in her voice and it scared me.

"How's Dad?" I asked.

"Dad? Oh, He's fine." She was acting a little strange.

"Doris, what's going on? Why are you so upset? If Dad's all right, I don't understand --"

"Oh, it is just my nerves, I guess. Frank is still out on the road. Warren and Darren have gone back to work. I've been sitting here all alone without my husband or brothers and feeling sorry for myself. Just to have you here means so much."

"Boy, you had me worried for a minute. Tell me about Dad. How serious is his problem, whatever it is?"

"Well, it isn't as serious as it might have been. He had appendicitis and it would have been a simple operation if he had told anyone when he first began having pain. But, by the time he asked for help, the appendix had ruptured. So that made it more complicated. He will have to rest and take it easy for awhile. I think they will let him go home in a couple of days -- if he has someone to stay with him for a while."

About that time, Dad began to squirm and wiggle around and finally opened his eyes.

"Who's here?" he asked. He had heard us talking.

"It's me, Dad, Angela." I rushed to his bed to put my arms around him.

He looked at me and smiled. "It was good of you to come, but I'm all right."

"I'm glad," I said. "But I had to see for myself. Now start getting better so they will let me take you home."

He smiled at me, and before we knew it, he drifted off to sleep again.

Doris said he still had a lot of medication in his system. She suggested that while he was sleeping we should go down to the hospital cafeteria for lunch.

~ ~ ~ ~ ~ ~ ~ ~ ~ ~ ~ ~ ~

Later that afternoon, when the doctor made his rounds, he checked Dad over carefully and asked several questions. "Seems this 'young man' is eager to leave this hospital. Well, I'll make a deal with you, Mr. Dobson. If you are doing this well tomorrow afternoon when I come by, we'll send you home the next morning. How's that?"

"Sounds great to me." Dad was quick to answer with a big smile on his face.

Since I was there, Doris decided to go home and rest a bit. Frank should be back later that evening. She looked exhausted.

After Doris left, Dad took another nap and I began to plan what I should do. I would spend the nights at Dad's house, and when they let him go home, I would stay a few days until he got stronger. It was only right that I should, and I had the time.

I needed to call Becky and report that all was well, and that I planned to stay a few days.

~ ~ ~ ~ ~ ~ ~ ~ ~ ~ ~ ~

After getting Dad settled at his house so he could rest, I went to the store for some supplies. He was going to need some nourishing food to rebuild his strength.

During the next few days, we were a couple of lazy people. The biggest chore was preparing the meals, but neither of us wanted much to eat. The rest of the time, we napped, watched TV, read, and talked a little about unimportant things.

At the end of a week, I took Dad in for a follow-up, and the report was good.

As we left the doctor's office and reached the car, Dad insisted on driving. "I'm doing so well, it's time for people to quit babying me. I'm a grown man, you know."

"Yes," I chuckle. "I seem to remember that from some time in the past. And I'm so thankful. You gave me quite a scare."

"Well, it was only appendicitis, you know. Not the plague. I admit it was kind of painful, but that type of surgery is quite simple nowadays."

We drove across town quietly for a few minutes. All the time I'm thinking how good it would be to have Dad come for a visit. Maybe then I could talk to him about everything.

"Dad, are you really feeling pretty good? Do you still get tired quickly? I need to get back home if I'm not needed here and I was thinking that, if you felt like it, you might want to come with me for a few days."

" M-m-m, well, I had thought I might like to do that, but I wasn't sure how you felt about it. You haven't said much about yourself since you've been here, except to tell me you aren't working right now. Made me wonder. Maybe if we had some time together --"

"Oh, good! How soon can you get ready? We will need to take your car. You know I came on the bus. Do you think you can drive that far?"

"Well, it will take only two or three hours, and if we get tired we can stop and rest. So let's plan on day after tomorrow. Okay?"

"Oh, yes! Very okay. I'll tell the others. I think that they will be relieved that we will be looking after each other. They don't seem to know what to make of me."

The trip home was practically uneventful. We stopped at a roadside café for lunch which consisted of a hamburger and coke, and arrived, safe and sound, about two o'clock. It feels so good to be home, but not alone.

Becky saw us drive in and dashed over to welcome me home and to meet Dad. She reported no excitement while I was away.

Chapter Twelve

I heard Dad moving around early the next morning. He has always been an early riser and he was eager to see everything.

So I got up as quickly as my aching body would allow, slipped on jeans and a shirt, and went to the kitchen. Dad was already there and had the coffee going. It didn't take long to scramble some eggs and make toast.

Then, things slowed down. We ate, talked about the pretty day, and how we slept last night. Dad was still tired from the trip and I wasn't too ambitious, so we just relaxed and drank our coffee.

"You've got a nice place here. A little help with the mowing and you should be able to handle it."

"Yes, I really like it, too. I want to put out some more flowers and a few shrubs. Maybe a tree, later. I'm thinking about that."

"The house is fairly new. Shouldn't be a lot of up-keep. While you do your 'woman stuff,' like the dishes and straightening the house, I think I'll take a little walk around just to get the lay of the land, you know."

"Sure, Dad. It's nice out and I want you to see everything. You may have some suggestions of things I should do to the house or grounds."

~ ~ ~ ~ ~ ~ ~ ~ ~ ~ ~ ~ ~

It is such a bright, sunny morning as I open the front door to let some sunshine into the living room. And the first thing I see is a cute little red head coming up the walk.

"Good Morning, Willie. How's things?"

"Great, Mrs. Graham."

"Oh, Willie, don't call me Mrs. Graham. We are better friends than that. My name is Angela."

"But I can't call you that. Mom says I must show respect to my elders, or she'll warm the seat of my pants."

"Well, we will have to think of something. You pick a name. I call you, Willie, not William Edward Rogers III. I had a nick name once, long ago, when I was a little girl."

"What was it? Can I call you by it? What do you think?"

"It was Missy. I see no reason why you can't use it. We're special friends after all."

"Thanks, Missy. That sounds good to me."

Just then, Dad rounded the corner of the house and saw Willie at the door.

"Dad, I'd like you to meet my special friend, Willie."

"Willie, this is my father, Mr. Dobson."

Willie put out his hand and they exchanged a firm handshake.

"Good to meet you," Dad said.

"You, too. You sure have a nice daughter. She is my special friend and my neighbor that God sent for me to love."

As I stood there with my mouth open, Dad reached out and put his arm around Willie's shoulder, saying, "Thanks, young man. You are an answer to my prayer." And they solemnly shook hands again.

"Well, I had better go," Willie said. "Some of the fellows are meeting down at the creek to look for tadpoles."

"What do you do with tadpoles when you catch them?" I asked.

"Oh, we hold them in our hands and watch them wiggle. Then we put them back into the water so they can grow up. Once I caught a minnow, but I had to put him back, too, so he could grow up."

"Sounds like fun. Just be careful. We don't want any boys falling in the creek."

"Okay." And off he goes skipping across the yard.

"That's quite a friend you have there," and Dad grins after him.

~ ~ ~ ~ ~ ~ ~ ~ ~ ~ ~ ~

After lunch, Dad takes me out and shows me a couple of places in the foundation of the house that need a little repair. He says he will check the phone book and find some one to do the job before he goes home.

I thank him because I never notice things like that. That's something else I'll have to start thinking about.

Then we talk a little about the flower beds, when suddenly, Dad stops and looks at me. "Angela, you look exhausted. Let's take a break. I could go for a nice cold glass of lemonade, if you happen to have one."

"Okay, a couple of glasses of lemonade in the shade on the back porch."

We sit quietly for a while, no one saying anything. Finally, "Good stuff, lemonade." This from Dad.

He sets his glass on the porch railing and turns to me, "Now, what's this about not working? Why not?"

I can't look at him, but I say, quietly, "Just couldn't handle the job any more."

"Wait a minute. What are you talking about? You are the best in the business. Everyone knows that. Have you let your grief get in the way?"

"Oh, Dad, you know working helped me. While I was concentrating on a project I didn't have time to think, or feel. How I wish I could work. But one cannot draw and sketch if she cannot see what she is doing."

"Can't see? What are you talking about, Girl?"

"Well, I have this disease called Macular Degeneration that is slowly, but surely destroying my sight. No one seems to know why it happens and there is no cure." I feel tears on my cheeks, and try to wipe them away. Then I feel Dad's arms around me, holding me close.

We just sit there for a while and I feel his sadness, too.

Suddenly he pulls away and says, "I just can't accept this. We'll find a doctor who knows what he's doing and we'll get this fixed!" He sounded almost angry.

"Sorry, Dad. I believe I have the best doctor in the business. I'd like you to meet him. I have an appointment on Friday. Would you go with me?"

"You bet I will! And we'll find out what's what. My little girl just can't be blind."

Chapter Thirteen

A slight tap on the door caused me to look up and see Becky with her hands full. I jumped up to open the door for her.

"What are you up to?" I ask.

"Oh, nothing much. I was fixing supper and thought of you. I know you are still tired from your trip, so I just made extra for you two."

"Oh, Becky, that is so kind of you. Here, let me help get those dishes to the kitchen."

When we return to the living room, Dad has put a smile on his face, but it is easy for me to see he is still disturbed. Becky seems to recognize it, too.

"Well, Mr. Dobson -- what do you think of our girl? She seems to be settling in pretty well, wouldn't you say?"

"Ah -- yes, Mrs. Rogers. She's done a fine job with the house. I really don't see how she has done so well considering her limited sight and facing blindness."

"What? I don't understand. Angela, what is he talking about?"

"Now don't get excited, Becky. I would have told you later. I just didn't want people to pity me, or feel sorry for me."

"Feel sorry for you? Oh, Angela -- and with the --"

A quick finger to my lips stops her in mid-sentence as she realizes she isn't the only one who doesn't have all the facts.

Becky puts her arms around me and says, "I'm so sorry. We'll talk later." Then, in a more normal tone, "Well, guess I had better go feed my brood. I just saw Eddie pulling into the driveway.

"Thanks, again," I say as she goes out the door.

Dad and I go to the kitchen where all that delicious food is waiting. I put out plates and silverware and fix something to drink.

Then we sit. And sit. I'm waiting for Dad to say the blessing, as he always does. But when I look up at him, all I can see are tears in his eyes.

Finally, he bows his head and says, softly, "Thank you, Lord, for this good food. You always supply all our needs. And we are grateful. Right now, I don't know just what to ask for, but please, bless my little girl and her sight. Please don't let her be blind." The "Amen" was mixed with tears.

We sit there for a while. Then I finally say, "Hey, this really looks good. And we need to eat. There is so much; we'll have plenty for tomorrow, too."

We did eat a little, then Dad said he would go look at the paper while I cleaned up.

~ ~ ~ ~ ~ ~ ~ ~ ~ ~ ~ ~ ~

The sun awoke me early, but as to be expected, Dad was already in the kitchen making coffee, and frying bacon. It smells good. After a quick, 'Good Morning,' I get the eggs and butter the toast.

The back door is open and the early morning sunshine is streaming across the floor, -- the promise of a beautiful day.

"How did you sleep?" he asks.

"Good," I say. It was the truth. I really got a good night's sleep.

"How about you?"

"Oh, about like you'd expect. When is that doctor's appointment?"

"Friday. Day after tomorrow. Now, Dad, you have to stop worrying about it. I'll figure out some way to handle it. I always do, when I have to. And we'll know more after talking with the doctor."

"Something's wrong here. It's not normal for a young woman to just suddenly go blind. I don't know what's going on, but I intend to find out."

I can think of no answer, so we finish our meal in silence.

As I begin clearing the dishes, Dad says a walk around the block might be good for him.

I agree. "And when you get back, maybe you can help me with that flower bed by the little storage building."

So off he goes on his walk. But he doesn't fool me. I know he is going in order to be by himself so he can pray. He's always done a lot of that, but this morning he is so troubled about my eyes. I know that's what's on his mind.

Quite some time later, I see Dad striding up the walk with a smile on his face. "It's going to be all right," he says. I've been praying about it. I don't know what the Lord has planned, but He will take care of you." He seemed so confident.

But I couldn't share his optimism. I'm the one losing sight, and God hasn't spoken to me. Since I no longer believe He cares about me, this is no comfort. Dad is just believing what he wants to be true. But I can't trust his "feelings."

We spent the rest of the day as well as the next day getting the flower beds in order and moving some spare things to the attic. Dad is busy and in a pretty cheerful frame of mind. But, now and then, I notice him slipping away by himself.

~ ~ ~ ~ ~ ~ ~ ~ ~ ~ ~ ~ ~

Friday morning, we go through the usual early morning routine, with Dad watching the clock.

"The doctor's appointment is not until ten o'clock," I remind him. But he seems eager to get on the way.

About nine-thirty I'm dressed and ready to go. Dad insists on driving, so I give directions. He appears to believe that after this meeting, some sort of magic will occur and I'll be fine again. I'm sorry that he's going to be let down.

Chapter Fourteen

I register at the main desk, and we wait in nearby chairs until my name is called.

Then a nurse indicates that it is my turn and takes me into the examining room. Dad follows.

After seating me in the chair, she makes small talk while putting drops into my eyes. Then she tells me the doctor will be with me shortly, and leaves. So we sit -- and wait.

The door opens quietly, and Dr. Wallace enters with a cheerful smile. He extends his hand, and we shake.

"Dr. Wallace, I would like you to meet my father, Russell Dobson. Dad, this is Dr. Kenneth Wallace."

They shake hands and Dr. Wallace asks Dad to be seated.

"I don't want to be in the way," Dad says.

"Of course, you won't be in the way. You may be interested in this examination. And we'll talk about any questions you may have."

"How are you doing?" the Doctor asks me.

"Fine," I say -- the usual reply.

"I'm glad to hear you say that, but I'm really interested in how you're adjusting to the idea of limited eyesight. The old saying that 'Attitude is everything,' is certainly true in making this adjustment. You can take the 'easy way,' just give up and depend on others to take care of you. Or, you can fight back and work out a system of your own so you can live a fairly normal life. I don't have to ask you which you will choose. I can tell that you are no quitter and will work hard to prove it to everyone. I will help you all I can."

"Now let's have a look and see how things have progressed since your last visit…"

We go through the procedure of adjusting my face to the equipment so he can begin the examination.

He is very careful, as usual, checking and rechecking. Then he releases me, pulls his chair back and seems to relax. And the cheerful smile appears again, and I wonder.

"Mrs. Graham, good news! There appears to be no change in he left eye at all, and if there is any in the right eye, it is very small. If this continues, it means that your degeneration is the slow-progressing type and you may have several years of relatively good sight. Of course, there are no guarantees. Things can change overnight. But for now, let's be hopeful."

"Doctor, I don't know what to say. My sight is definitely not normal. I have problems. Yet, I'm happy you believe it may not get much worse anytime soon. That does encourage me."

"All right. Let's think of some things that may help for the time being. As you go about your housework, wear some type of mask over your left eye. No, don't try to read. Just do routine house work. This will cause you to depend on the peripheral vision of your right eye. Of course, this should be for short periods of time, until you become accustomed to it. I think you will find this helps you to move about and do routine things with more confidence."

"There is one more thing I would suggest. I have a friend, Dr. Randy Lymon, who specializes in prescribing glasses for people with low vision. I believe he can help. When you stop at the desk to make your next appointment with me, the receptionist will give you a card with his name, address, and phone number. After thinking about it, you may want to call him and make an appointment. We're just trying to make you more comfortable, and help you to function at your best."

"Thank you, Doctor. You are so very kind. I believe your purpose is to help me. I'm grateful. I can tell you I'm much more hopeful than when I left here the last time."

"Frankly, Mrs. Graham, I am, too. I think we should visit once a month for now, and we'll see how things go."

"That sounds good too me. Ah -- Doctor, I think my Father would like to speak with you, if you have the time."

"Certainly, Mr. Dobson, how can I help?"

"Well, Doctor, I have to tell you that when I came here, I was pretty upset and determined to demand that everything possible be done to help my daughter. But as I watched you and listened to your advice, I realized that you are taking this problem very seriously and are doing everything possible to help. I'm very relieved and have great confidence in you. I'm sorry I misjudged you and the situation."

"Oh, I understand your feelings, Mr. Dobson. I get frustrated at times because I can't do more. However a great amount of work and research is going on constantly, and one day we will have some good answers for this kind of problem. I pray for it and believe it will happen."

"I'll join you in that prayer. I can see my child is in good hands."

We all shake hands and Dad and I go out to make my next appointment.

Chapter Fifteen

On the way home, Dad wants to stop at the tree nursery. There are a couple of things he wants to add to the backyard.

I'm surprised to see that he chose a young oak and a maple. I know it will take years for them to grow, but I'm very pleased. In my imagination, I can see a swing hanging from a branch and a young girl swinging back and forth in the summer breeze.

Dad spends the next couple of days planting the trees and puttering around the yard, and then decides it's time for him to go home.

He seems more comfortable with my failing sight, almost as if isn't happening. I know the doctor was very encouraging, and while I appreciate his help, I am still very fearful of losing what sight I still have.

But Dad prays, and acts as if the prayer has already been answered. So there's no use to talk to him about my fears. As usual, I'll just have to figure out a way to make it on my own.

After Dad leaves, the house suddenly seems so empty. And I realize I didn't mention to him that I'm going to have a baby. I guess it is just as well. It would give him something else to worry about and "pray" about. He'll know about it when the time comes.

~ ~ ~ ~ ~ ~ ~ ~ ~ ~ ~ ~ ~

It occurs to me, that while Becky has visited me several times, I have never been to her house. So I give her a call and she says to come on over.

Becky meets me in dust cap and mittens. "Sit," she says. " I'm just about through here and I'll be with you in a minute."

Then we decide to sit on the porch swing and enjoy the freshness of the morning.

"Okay," she says. "Let's have it. What's this about the blindness your father mentioned?"

"Well, it's pretty simple, as I understand it. I have Macular Degeneration, which destroys the nerves of the central vision. I'm told I will never be in complete darkness, but with peripheral vision, I will be able to find my way around and be, more or less, independent. I just won't be able to read, write, or sketch. Could be worse, right?" And suddenly I start to cry.

Becky holds me for a minute, then pulls back and looking straight at me, says, "You're right. It could be a lot worse. And with your spunk, I know you will find a way to live with it."

"Oh, Becky, you just don't understand. How can I take care of a baby when I can't even look directly into its face? How will I make sure I'm giving the right medication? Oh, there are so many potential problems, and I don't have any answers."

"Well, for one thing -- the baby isn't here yet. You have some time to work on these things and develop plans. And you're not alone, you know. I'll be around to help if you need me. Most of all our Heavenly Father will guide you. I was often amazed when our children were young and I was confused about how to handle a situation, if I prayed about it, God always gave me the answer. I didn't know how to be a mother and rear children. But each day, I asked God to guide me. And I'll be praying for you too."

"Well, that's kind of you, Becky. I know I can depend on you. And pray if you want to, but you know I don't have any faith in that. Between the two of us, we'll work it out."

"How did your father react when you told him about the baby?"

"Oh, I guess we never got around to talking about the baby. Dad was so upset about my sight until he talked with the doctor. Then he calmed down and did some things to make it easier for me. Even planted two trees in the back yard. I appreciated all he did, but we know he can't take care of me all my life. I have to handle my life my own way, so I didn't want to give him something else to worry about."

"Oh, Angela, you are a mess. But I love you. Between Willie and me, we'll get you on the right track one of these days. Which reminds me, what's this about Willie calling you 'Missy'? He claims it is a nickname and he's allowed to use it."

"Well, yes, we had a little discussion a few days ago. We are good friends, you know. He's not just 'any little kid.' And I call him Willie, not William Edward Rogers III. So we agreed he should call me by my nickname."

"Well, I guess it's all right. I just want my children to be polite and respectful."

"That's one thing you don't have to worry about. Becky, you are a wonderful mother. I hope I can be like you."

Chapter Sixteen

The days pass slowly. The regular morning housework doesn't take long when one lives alone.

I've taken a few walks around the neighborhood and find that I enjoy the exercise and fresh air. Helps me get a better perspective of where I live. The neighbors seem friendly. They always smile and speak. But I never stop to chat. That's just not my style. I'm sure we have nothing in common to talk about.

If only I could see better so I could read, or sketch. Maybe I should investigate those glasses for people of low vision. I certainly qualify.

~ ~ ~ ~ ~ ~ ~ ~ ~ ~ ~ ~ ~

I'm so glad Dr. Wallace referred me to his friend, Dr. Lymon. It's amazing how much difference it makes with these glasses which he prescribed.

And I was impressed with the viewing machine Dr. Lymon demonstrated. I'm really considering getting one. It would enable me to do some things to keep my mind busy while waiting.

Uh, oh, that reminds me that it is time to check back with my obstetrician to make sure Tater Tot is doing all right.

~ ~ ~ ~ ~ ~ ~ ~ ~ ~ ~ ~ ~

"Good Morning, Mrs. Graham. Good to see you."

"Good Morning, Doctor Kradel. It's good to see you, too."

"You're looking well. How are you feeling?"

"Physically, I'm fine. The morning sickness has subsided, and while I seem to be a little low on energy, I'm managing quite well. Emotionally, well, that is something else. I guess I'm not prepared to handle this alone. It would be so different if Chuck were still alive. We would have a lot of happy plans. But as it is, I'm tired, confused and uncertain about how I can manage. I know this sounds pretty self-centered, and I guess I am. I'm just not prepared to be an only parent, - - alone."

"Of course I understand how you might feel that way. But I must assure you that you will not have to handle this all by yourself. I plan to be on the job for some time and will do everything I can to help. I'm sure you have family and friends who will be glad to lend a hand. And, most of all, our Heavenly Father will guide you as you ask for His help day by day."

"That's a nice little speech, Doctor. But you don't know me very well. I have always been a very independent person except for the time of my marriage. We two were one and depended entirely on each other. My Dad, my sister and my brothers are good people but we have very little in common with each other. I have one friend, a neighbor who lives across the street. She has her own family to care for. So you see, I must continue to be independent."

"As for what God might do for me, I'm pretty uncertain about that. He let me down years ago when He took my Mother just when I needed her the most. So we've had very little dealings with each other since then. I need a God I can trust, but I don't believe there is one."

"WOW! You've got it all figured out, haven't you? I can tell you have given this some thought. I'm afraid, however, that you have been thinking in the wrong direction. But I'm not one to argue with you about your relationships with others and with God. That is your decision. But I would be miserable, too, if that were my philosophy."

"Let's check you out and see how you are doing, physically. I see you aren't gaining too much weight. That's good. Just make sure you eat a healthy diet, for as you have often heard, you are eating for two. And the nourishment the child gets before birth, helps him, or her, get a good start in life."

"Now everything seems to be in order. I'd say you are doing fine. Keep up the good work, and before long, we'll deliver a strong, healthy baby."

"Do you have children, Doctor?"

He looks up from his note pad and seems to stare at me for a moment. There appears a sad expression in his eyes. "No, sorry. I don't. My wife and I love children and had big plans. But my wife is very fragile and her health will not allow it. We considered adoption, but, again, her health would prevent her caring for a child. I'm sorry. I don't usually share this with patients. But we've talked about personal things and feelings today. I'll be more professional in the future."

"No need to apologize. I'm the one who started this discussion, I'm afraid. You are very easy to talk with. Thank you. I'm still following your instructions. See you in a month."

As I leave, the Doctor continues to sit at his desk, staring at the note pad. I doubt he noticed I was gone.

Chapter Seventeen

The days come and go. I finally have the house in pretty good order. I stand in the middle of the little empty bedroom and try to envision how it should look, how it should be arranged to be most convenient.

The lone piece of furniture, a rocking chair, is conveniently at hand, and I find myself sitting, rocking, and thinking. I wonder how my Mother felt before I was born. Of course, she had Daddy and the other kids. And a strong faith. That would be nice, I think. But it is not for me.

Now that I've learned I will be able to see, at least, a little, I feel more confident that I can care for a baby. I've read some of the material that was handed to me at the doctor's office. Maybe I'll learn, in time. I feel such a sense of responsibility, and yet I feel so incompetent. I hope I don't mess up on this. I've never had anyone to care for before. I want to be a good mother, I really do. I just don't know how.

Becky keeps telling me that God will lead me and guide me. Sure wish I had her faith. But past experience tells me this is yet another time I must learn to depend on myself, alone.

Even Dr. Mike mentioned God for comfort and help. And Dad always goes to God. I don't understand where all these people get these great ideas. It's plain to see that God has never turned His back on them like He has on me. Well, time will tell, I guess.

Chapter Eighteen

"Hello?" "Well, Good morning to you."

"Oh, Becky, Good morning to you, too."

"Got any big plans for the day?"

"Nothing too exciting. Why?"

"Seems to me it is about time to start working on the nursery. What color are you going to paint it? Blue or pink?"

"Oh, I don't know. I like baby blue, but a girl might not like that."

"How about painting the walls a light blue and using pink in the decorations?"

"That sounds great. The next time you are going down town, let know and I'll go with you and buy the paint. The sooner I get started, the sooner I'll finish."

"That's why I called. I'm going to the 'Home' store to look for some light fixtures for the bath room, so I thought you might want to look for paint there."

"Wonderful. Thank you."

~ ~ ~ ~ ~ ~ ~ ~ ~ ~ ~ ~ ~

"Now, Becky, I can handle this. I've never painted walls before, but I'm sure I can figure it out. Glad you knew what equipment I would need."

"Okay, I'll just supervise. First, we need to give the paint a good stir and pour some into this pan. While you start the walls, I'll put tape around the windows and door. Now, hold the handle like this and give firm, smooth stokes. Up and down. Cover all surfaces --"

"Hey, Supervisor, give that to me and get on with your tape."

"Okay, but I like to paint. When I get the taping done, I'll grab that brush and we'll be finished in no time."

So we spent the afternoon putting a pretty blue color on Tater Tot's room. It really looks good. I can't wait to get some furniture.

~ ~ ~ ~ ~ ~ ~ ~ ~ ~ ~ ~ ~

In the meantime, I must visit Dr. Wallace again. Seeing two doctors every month keeps me going and coming. I really don't think it is necessary, but I'm afraid not to go.

"Good Morning, Doctor," as he shakes my hand. Then I assume the usual position in the chair, so he can shine that bright light into my eyes again.

He smiles as he pulls back and removes the equipment. "Things are still looking good," he says. I assume you are still using the medication and not doing anything to cause eye strain."

"You assume right, Doctor Wallace. I'm almost afraid to read the newspaper."

"Well, so far, so good. Of course, I'm pleased with the way your eyes are behaving. But I fear this won't continue forever and I want to be realistic as we discuss this problem. There is a lot of research going on today in the field of Macular Degeneration. Of course, the ideal would be to find a way to prevent it, but that is proving to be very difficult. However the medical researchers aren't giving up in looking for ways to treat it. Some day there will be a break through, and I hope it will be soon enough to be of benefit to you and my other patients. It's really frustrating not to be able to give the help you need. But as I say, for now, you are doing fine. Try not to worry, and keep hoping. Just keep trusting that God will take care of you, one way or the other."

There was that word, "God," again. I smile, but inside I feel cold, excluded, and rejected. We shake hands again as I leave and make my next appointment.

Chapter Nineteen

I've just turned the corner into the front yard, checking the flower beds for stray grass and weeds, when I sense someone standing behind me. I turn quickly -- and see Willie with a big grin on his face.

"Did I scare you, Missy?"

"Well, not exactly. I would probably say, 'surprised me.'"

"Are you working hard? Maybe I could help."

"Well, it isn't hard work, except I have to bend over and that's not easy. But you are a lot closer to the ground than I am, so I would appreciate your help. Just pull the grass and weeds and toss them aside. I'll gather them up later."

"Is it hard to bend over because you are going to have a baby?"

"Yes, that makes it harder, but how did you know that?"

"I heard Mom talking to Dad about using the pickup truck to bring some furniture for your baby's room. And since you don't have a baby, I figured you must be going to have one."

"I see. Smart figuring on your part. But it will be a while yet."

"Then will your baby's Daddy come home and help take care of it?"

"Willie, let's go get a glass of lemonade and sit in the porch swing for a little while. You can finish the flower beds later."

So we did.

~ ~ ~ ~ ~ ~ ~ ~ ~ ~ ~ ~

"Willie, you remember when I moved here, I didn't have any family and I was very sad. I still am. My husband, the baby's father, had been killed in a bad automobile accident. I felt so alone. Still do a lot of the time. But

I have the baby to look forward to, and you, my young friend, have been a great help."

As I tousled his hair, I muttered, "That cute little grin of yours gives me hope."

"I'm glad. And I can be a big help taking care of the baby. I helped a lot taking care of Jean. Is your baby going to be a girl or a boy?"

"Well, we don't know that yet. But we'll love it, whoever it is."

"Yes, God knows who you need and he already knows who it is."

"Oh, Willie, I --"

"Yeah, I know. You don't seem to think much of God. I don't know why. He is so good to you and loves you and all. I keep praying and asking Him to make you understand."

"Well, Willie, I guess it's time for us to get back to our grass pulling."

"Oh, I almost forgot. I came to ask you to go with us to church tomorrow night. All us kids who went to camp are going to stand up front and tell what we did and learned, and all. It'll be great. I have a good story I want you to hear. Will you come?"

"Oh, Willie, I don't know. I don't feel much like going out at night. Couldn't you just tell me your story now?"

"Oh, no. It wouldn't be as good. And besides other kids have something to tell you, too."

"Let me think about it. What time are you going?"

"The program starts at seven o'clock so we will probably go about twenty minutes before that. Please say you will go."

"Willie, you are my friend, so if it is that important to you, I'll try to go. I don't know any other reason I'm doing this."

~ ~ ~ ~ ~ ~ ~ ~ ~ ~ ~ ~

There was a large crowd at the church. As time drew near for the service to start, people began to settle down and get quiet. I sat with Becky, Ed, and Jean, as we waited.

The pastor walked out and stood behind the pulpit, and three young boys followed him, and sat in chairs that had been placed there.

Following a prayer, the pastor began to talk about the church camp. For those who were not familiar with the camp, he told its location, the number of youngsters who attended, and a few things about the activities.

Then he looked at the boys sitting beside him. "These three young fellows have volunteered to tell you more about the camp and their experiences of the week. Timothy will be the first to speak. --Tim --"

Timothy stood up, and grinned at everybody. "I sure had a good time," he said. "And I want to thank you all for having a camp like that so we could go. I lived in the city, before, you know. And never had enough money to go to camp, like some of the kids did. So this was great. I guess the most fun for me were the baseball games, or maybe it was the swimming in the creek. It was neat having someone to show me how to swim and give me a chance to learn. It was a fun time. Hope I get to go next year. Thank you."

There was a nice round of applause as Tim sat down with a big grin on his face.

Then it was Tommy's time. He did a good job of telling about the fun he had and thanking everybody. He also said Brother Johnny was a special friend to all of them and was good at explaining the Bible to them. The crowd gave him a big hand.

The pastor spoke, "Well, Willie, looks like you're last, son. Tell us what the camp meant to you."

So Willie stood up and looked right at me and then his family. "I'm glad I get to tell you about what camp did for me this year. I know you think it is important for us kids, to get out in the country for a week and have a good time in the sunshine and fresh air. And we sure did!" (Wide grin, slapping his right hand into the palm of the left, like he was hitting his glove with the ball.) "My team won at least one game every day, and one day, we won both of them. And we had good eats, too. Thanks to all the Moms who sent food."

Then he paused, looking at the floor, then looked up directly at me. I know I didn't imagine it. He was trying to tell me something.

"But the best part of camp for me this year wasn't the fun and food. Something special happened to me. We were in the prayer circle Wednesday night, and after we prayed, Brother Johnny started telling us a story."

"It wasn't a new story. We had heard it before. But he told us how Baby Jesus was born in Bethlehem and grew up to die on the cross. Then he began to ask us why Jesus died. Some said because the soldiers were mean and they liked to kill people. And somebody else said He died because that was what He was supposed to do. And some said some other things. But suddenly, I knew why Jesus died. He did it for me! So I could be God's child and go to Heaven. And I was so (a few sobs slipped out and a tear rolled down his cheek) ashamed that I hadn't always done what I should, and one time I did something I shouldn't, and Dad found out about it and gave me a spanking, and all that stuff. Right then, I knew I had to ask God to forgive me because Jesus died for me. And He did!" (Now there was a big smile on that tear stained face). "He forgave me right then, and I even felt different. Makes me wish everyone would ask God to forgive them because Jesus died for them, too."

"Well, I had a great time at camp and I thank you for letting us go, and I'll always remember this summer when God saved me at camp. Thank you."

As Willie sat down, there was clapping, and handkerchiefs wiping tears from faces. And I just felt awful. Right then I knew Jesus died for me too, and long ago, God had saved me. But I hadn't lived for Him.

But, then, I also felt He was the one who had turned His back on me, taking away those I loved and causing me to have to get by on my own. I was glad for Willie. But my situation hadn't changed.

Chapter Twenty

Another visit to Dr. Kradel proved that all is well with my pregnancy and moving along according to plan.

Becky and I have finished the nursery and I must admit it is quite attractive. It will be nice too have someone living there.

I read in the paper that there will be an exhibition, or showing of some of that new communicating equipment -- computers. I've read about "Big Bertha," but it's hard to realize they now have a device that can contain all that information in a machine small enough that we could have one in our homes. The exhibit will be Wednesday and Thursday next week at the Convention Center.

Becky and I are going to the exhibit and then have lunch at the Deli. She is such a wonderful friend. I don't know how I would get through these days without her.

~ ~ ~ ~ ~ ~ ~ ~ ~ ~ ~ ~ ~

It's time for the fall clothes to be at market. I wonder who did that new line after I left? I need to go see Mr. Whitman, just to keep in touch.

Perhaps Friday would be the best day. Fridays are usually slower, unless it is in the middle of a rush season.

But what will I say to him? He doesn't even know about Tater Tot. I just need to keep in touch a little.

~ ~ ~ ~ ~ ~ ~ ~ ~ ~ ~ ~ ~

Ah, the place looks the same. And the work rooms are humming. I'd better check in at the desk before going to Mr. Whitman's office.

"Hello, Penny."

"Yes." She looks up. "Angela!" she squeals. "Let me look at you -- Uh, oh, I didn't know."

"Yeah, well, I didn't either when I saw you last. But it must have happened just a few weeks before Chuck's death." And suddenly, my voice isn't very steady.

"Oh, that's wonderful! Now you won't be alone. I'm so happy for you. How are your eyes?"

"A little worse than they were, but not as bad as I had expected them to be by this time. I still drive a little, if I'm careful."

"Do you think I could see Mr. Whitman?"

"Of course. I'd better not let you get out of here without seeing him. He was so lost without you. Nothing worked out the way it should after you left. Even some days, now, we tip-toe around like scared mice. Just go tap on his door and go in."

"Yes?"-- Come in. -- Ah -- Oh! Angela, come in, girl. Let me look at you." As he rushes forward, and holds me close -- then pulls away and takes a long look.

"Oh, my! Girl, you didn't tell me about this."

"No. I didn't know about it the last time I saw you. It was a surprise to me, too. Must have happened just before Chuck's death. I'm due in November."

"Well, that's wonderful, of course. But I was hoping you had come back to work. How are the eyes doing?"

"Actually, the doctor thinks I'm doing very well considering that I have Macular Degeneration in both eyes. He says it is developing slowly, so I should be able to manage for some time."

"Well, that's good news -- I think. But it doesn't give me much hope of getting you back here at work."

"I'm trying to look forward, one day at a time. I will have a baby to care for. I just don't know what to expect. But I've always worked things out in the past, so I'm sure I will this time."

"Oh, I'm sure you will do an excellent job with your child as you have with everything else. But we really need you. This is a tough business these days."

"I'm sure it is. And I would love to be here, but I know you understand."

"Yes, I do. But keep in touch. You never know when things might change."

"It's been good visiting with you, Mr. Whitman, and I will probably see you again when I have someone new for you to meet. I just wanted to thank you for the financial help you have provided. It has really made a difference."

"I'm glad. But you don't owe me any thanks. You earned it. Now take good care of yourself."

~ ~ ~ ~ ~ ~ ~ ~ ~ ~ ~ ~

I guess I had better do the rest of my errands and go home. It will soon be rest time.

Chapter Twenty-One

This is the day Becky and I are going to see those new computers. They fascinate me. I can hardly wait to see a demonstration.

~ ~ ~ ~ ~ ~ ~ ~ ~ ~ ~ ~ ~

"My, what a big building. I guess this is the main entrance. Let's have a look."

"Now, Angela, I don't mind looking. Probably be interesting, but I can't see any practical use for a machine like that."

"Well, we don't know much about it. That's why we're here. We might learn something. Oh, look! That man is talking to a group of people. Let's see what's going on."

"-- And now, Ladies and Gentlemen, if you will just line up so we can go one at a time. You, Sir, will you sit at this desk and look at the screen in front of you. You see listed a number of personal questions: Your name, address, height, weight, your favorite food and what you do to relax. Please type your answers in the appropriate spaces. Next, you will walk over here and accept the card from the key punch operator, then insert the card into this "reader" machine. Out comes the list. Are these the answers you put into the machine?"

"All kinds of information can be put on these little cards and stored in a small place, yet be available for retrieval years later. This wonderful machine can be adapted to fit your individual business. Saves time. Makes money. Now, let me explain --"

"Come on, Angela. I've seen enough for one day."

"You mean you don't want to save time and make money. I don't understand you," I chuckle.

We go back to our shopping. But I can't get that machine out of my head. Some day, I'm going to have one and learn to use it, just to see what I can do.

~ ~ ~ ~ ~ ~ ~ ~ ~ ~ ~ ~

I pick up my mail as I go into the house and drop it on the hall table. After putting away my purchases, I make a small glass of lemonade, kick off my shoes, and sit in the recliner. Ah, it feels good to be home and just sit down. After a time, I manage to get up and grab the mail before falling back into my chair. Two catalogs, as usual, the Shopper's Special, a legal-looking envelope and a card reminding me that my next appointment with Dr. Wallace is on Monday. I rise up and put the card on the mantle where I will be sure to see it.

The return address on the legal envelope is:

Smith, Jones, & Brown, Attorneys at Law
6547 East Concord
St. Louis, MO

Never heard of them.

The brief letter inside reads:

Dear Mrs. Graham:

It has been brought to our attention that you are the widow of Charles David Graham, a former client of ours. We were not notified of his death and only recently learned that he is deceased. May we express our sincere sympathy to you in your loss. We have managed your late husband's financial portfolio for several years and need to meet with you to bring our files up to date and inform you of the details of our agreement with him. Will you please call our office, at the above number, and suggest a time that will be convenient time for you to meet, and I will call on you and explain his affairs.

Sincerely,
Thomas H. Brown
Attorney at Law

Wow! What a shock. What is he talking about? I suppose those papers in the Safe Deposit Box might explain. But I didn't pay much attention to them when I was looking for Chuck's life insurance policy and the Deed to the house. I was pretty confused at the time and I had planned to go back and go through everything. But with all that has happened, I never gave it another thought.

Well, I guess we need to find out what Mr. Brown has to say. I'll phone his office and ask him to stop by tomorrow. Things will be moving pretty fast in the next few weeks, so I may as well get this in order and out of the way.

~ ~ ~ ~ ~ ~ ~ ~ ~ ~ ~ ~ ~

"Good Afternoon, Mr. Brown. I'm Angela Graham. Please come in."

"I'm pleased to meet you, Mrs. Graham. Where would you like for us to talk?"

"In the living room, if that is all right with you."

"Mrs. Graham, I'm sorry for your loss and sorry we didn't contact you sooner, but we only learned of Mr. Graham's death when we recently called his office at the firm where he worked. He had always been so prompt to give us regular interviews about his affairs, so when he missed two appointments, we became concerned."

"I understand, and I hope you understand why I didn't contact you. I'm sure Chuck had intended to explain all his affairs to me in time, but we both worked at demanding jobs, and when we had a little time for ourselves, the subject just never came up."

"He did leave a Will. Both of us had Wills drawn up shortly after our marriage. And I'm sure there are papers in our Safe Deposit Box pertaining to your relationship with him. Frankly, I was in shock. Everything happened so unexpectedly. I just took out the papers I needed at the time and forgot about the rest."

"I certainly understand, Mrs. Graham. Among other things, we are in possession of Deeds to several pieces of property in the City and surrounding areas. The instructions we have are to manage the funds and maintain the properties until he called for them. We assumed he would let us know if there was an emergency need for the funds, or, if at some point, he would like to set aside a retirement fund. If he did not call for the assets prior to his death, we were to maintain them in trust for the family he left behind. In order to begin the process we need certified copies of your marriage license, and birth certificates for each child."

"I will be glad to have a copy of the marriage license made, and I will drop it off at your office next Monday when I am in the area to visit my Ophthalmologist. However, as you can see, we will have to wait a while for a copy of the baby's birth certificate."

"That will be fine. In the meantime, we will continue with our previous instructions in maintaining the assets. It will all work out in time."

"Mrs. Graham, (extending his hand for a shake) please feel free to ask us for any help that we may be able to give you. We will see you in a few days."

He was out the door, and I stood there, wondering what had just happened and what it would mean in the future.

Chapter Twenty-Two

After leaving a copy of my marriage license with the attorney, I arrived at the doctor's office for my regular eye check-up.

"Angela Graham to see Dr. Wallace."

"Yes -- you may go in now."

So I sit in the outer office with one other patient, a man, who is absorbed in a magazine. The nurse soon comes for him, leaving me alone to sit and think.

I am not prepared for the imminent future. I will be having my baby soon, and although I have its room ready and an adequate supply of clothing and other necessities, I'm really not prepared to care for a newborn.

It almost frightens me to realize that I will be responsible for a young life. Oh, if Chuck were only here! We could work this out together. I feel so alone.

Perhaps I should get Dad to come stay with us for a while until I get educated about caring for a new baby.

The nurse returns and takes me to the doctor's office. While she is applying all the drops in my eyes, we have a few friendly words. I ask if she has children, and she tells me she has two.

That gets me to the place where I can ask, "How do you handle those first few days?"

She grins, and says, "Getting cold feet? Too late to back out now."

"You're quite right. But I'm afraid I won't know what to do or how to do it."

"Don't worry. It's the most normal thing in the world. Maybe your

Mother can come visit a few days. I remember that I prayed a lot. God does help, you know. You'll be fine."

I did not respond when she mentioned mother. Oh, how I long for her.

The nurse finished her work left, saying, "The doctor will be with you in a few minutes."

'So God is going to help me? Oh, sure. Just like He has always helped me. I guess if people don't know anything practical to say, that's an easy way out.'

I'm startled as the Doctor greets me. "Hello, Mrs. Graham." I look up to see his smiling face.

"Sorry," I say. "Just thinking."

"Most people say that is a good practice," he grins. "Now let's see how things are with you."

So we go through the regular routine of the examination of both eyes, and he checks the records from the last examination.

"M- m - m ," he ponders. Then turning too me, he says, "Well, things look pretty good. Not as good as we would like, of course, but, actually, much better than I had expected by this time, when I first examined you. The problem continues, of course. But the progression is very slow, so that gives us hope that the new medical trials will provide us with something to help. You are aware that constant research continues and some scientists are expecting a break-through very soon. I don't want to give you any false hope, but I am confident that the time will come when help is available. We must trust that God will keep you on track until that happens."

"For now, I suggest you continue as you have been. You are doing remarkably well. We certainly have reason to thank God and trust His continued help. How are you feeling, otherwise?"

"Large, Doctor." I smile. "I'm doing fine. But I may have to miss my next appointment with you if the delivery of my baby goes according to plan."

"I understand. As things stand now with your eyes, missing a visit here wouldn't be too tragic. You can let me know. If you have no further problems, we will just shift you over to the next regular appointment."

I rise, and he extends his hand. We shake and he gives me a reassuring smile. And I'm out of there and on my way.

~ ~ ~ ~ ~ ~ ~ ~ ~ ~ ~ ~

On the way home, I ponder the idea of calling Dad. I feel like I really do need him at this time. Oh, I could hire someone to stay with me a few weeks after the baby's birth. But I would feel a lot more comfortable with Dad, and I think he deserves this opportunity.

Of course, he will be surprised. I feel a little guilty for not telling him about the baby, sooner. But I guess it wouldn't have changed anything. He will have plenty of time to adjust in the next month or so.

~ ~ ~ ~ ~ ~ ~ ~ ~ ~ ~ ~ ~

After kicking off my shoes and getting a cold drink, I lean back in the recliner and pick up the phone. He answers on the first ring - - .

"Hello. Dad? Angela."

"Hello, My dear. Is everything all right?"

"Yes, I'm fine. How about you? Are you feeling Okay? Got the house and yard in good shape?"

"I'm doing really well and things look pretty good right now. All the leaves are raked and mulched. The plants are trimmed back, ready for winter. Even had a load of firewood delivered yesterday. Just abut ready to settle back and catch up on my reading."

"Well, I am calling to ask if you would like to come for a visit -- a week, or two? You can bring your reading along. And I'll let you do a little leaf raking in my yard, if you want exercise."

"Angela, what's up? You know I would love to see you and spend a little time with you. But I wasn't expecting this invitation."

"I know it is a little unusual. But I thought it might help to have you here for a while. I have a little surprise for you, Dad. It's almost time for me to deliver your new grandchild, and I thought you might want to be here."

"Angela, what in the world are you talking about?"

"I know I should never have kept this from you, Dad, but there never seemed to be a right time to tell you. And I knew you would worry. So, I just didn't mention it. I've done quite well. No major problems. But I need to have you here when the time comes."

"All right. That's all I need to know now. I'll call Doris and your brothers and tell them I'm going to visit you. We'll wait and surprise them later, if that's all right with you."

"That sounds good, Dad. But don't start out this minute. We have plenty of time. Wait and come Monday morning, after you have rested over the weekend. I'm looking forward to having you here."

"Yes, and I am looking forward to being there, too. You've got a lot of explaining to do, Young Lady. I'm eager to see you. I'll call before I leave, so you'll know I'm on the way. Bye, now."

Chapter Twenty-Three

After breakfast, I sit and ponder my day. Saturday morning with an extra cup of coffee is an old American custom. I guess the first order of business is to make sure Dad's room is ready for him. I've tried to keep it neat, but a little dusting and rearranging, here and there won't hurt. And I had better check the pantry and refrigerator. I probably need to make a quick trip to the market. But after that, I'll be all set, so I can be lazy for a couple of days, until he gets here. I'll start that new novel I've been intending to read. Then, maybe late this afternoon, if it isn't too cold, I might try to visit Becky for a few minutes. I haven't been there in a while and I may not have another chance soon.

After clearing breakfast dishes and putting the kitchen to rights, I check Dad's room. Then I sit down and make my list for the store.

"Missy?" -- Oh, oh. I hear a familiar voice.

"Come in, Willie. I'm in the kitchen. Oh, you look bright and shiny this morning, young man. A special occasion?"

"No, I just got cleaned up and decided to get out of Mom's way while she is doing her week-end baking. Jean thinks she's helping, but I know it would be a lot easier if Mom didn't have to explain everything to her. She's planning on being a great cook some day, so I guess I can plan on eating. I'm petty good at that."

"Well, if you don't have any thing better to do, how about going to the store with me? I'm having company next week. My Dad is coming to stay a while."

"Hey, that's great. I really like him and we have good, long talks together. Will he be here long?"

"Yes, several weeks, I think. He wants to be here when Tater-Tot arrives."

"Oh, is he coming next week, too?"

"I don't think so. But Dad and I will have a few days to visit before he -- or she arrives."

~ ~ ~ ~ ~ ~ ~ ~ ~ ~ ~ ~ ~

"Thanks for helping me with my groceries, Willie. But I expect your Mother will be looking for you for lunch about now. Maybe you can come back again later."

"Okay, see you. -- Oh! I almost forgot the main reason I came to see you. I wanted to ask you to go to Sunday School and Church with us in the morning. It is Promotion Day and I'm moving up to the next class. I'm eight now, you know. They are going to have us line up in front of the people and give us a CERTIFICATE! Won't that be grand? And since you are my best friend, I want you to be there so you can be proud of me."

"Willie, you know I'm always proud of you. You are one of the best people I know. But I don't think I can go. You're always thinking up ways to get me to church. I know you mean well, but I'm a hopeless case. Don't waste your time worrying about me. You know how I feel about God. He doesn't care about me."

"Missy, that's not true. Whenever I talk to God about you, I can just feel, deep down inside, that He wants me to get you back to church. I know He loves you."

"Oh, Willie. You just don't understand. I love you, my young friend, and it hurts to see those tears in your eyes. But it is just best that I learn to depend on myself and not get hurt again."

"Don't look so sad, Dear. I'm proud of you for being promoted and I wouldn't hurt you for the world. Maybe God is different with you. But I know how He feels about me, so I'll just not bother Him. I do thank you for caring, but just forget about me as far as God is concerned."

"You know I can't do that. You are my best friend and I --" He turns and runs out the door with tears streaming down his face.

I feel terrible. Willie is such a good little fellow. And it is sweet that he cares so much. I don't want to hurt him. But I just can't afford to get side-tracked on God again.

Oh, well, he'll get over it, in time. As he gets older, he'll see why I feel the way I do.

Guess I'll start that new book. M-m-m- let's see who wrote it. Oh, I've read her books before. She's always good.

The phone rings, and as I pick it up and say "Hello," I hear Becky's voice.

"Angela, do you know what's wrong with Willie? He came in, and when I asked where he had been, he told me he went to the store with you. Then he looked like he was going to cry, and turned around and ran into his room and closed the door. "I'm preparing to go in and talk to him. But I wanted to check with you first. Did he get into trouble? What's he done now?"

"Oh, no, Becky. You know he doesn't get into trouble. It's all my fault and I feel terrible about it, but I just can't pretend to be something I'm not."

"Somehow Willie thinks it is his mission in life to get me back in church. He is always trying to find a way to get me to go to church with your family. During our visit today, he mentioned that he wanted me to go for Promotion Day because he is going to get a Certificate. I think that's great, but then, I'd have to sit through a sermon and that makes me uncomfortable and I just told him I couldn't go, and that he should forget about trying to get God and me together."

"Wow! Now I understand the tears. The poor child does think you are his mission. He really loves you, but he can't understand why you don't want to be close to God and let Him love and care for you. A child's faith is so simple. It's a shame we sometimes outgrow it. Well, thanks. I'll talk to him and we'll work it out. I know how he feels, but I'm just praying God will touch your heart when you are ready. Please don't hold this against him. Willie really does care for you."

"Oh, Becky. I'm so sorry. I love Willie, too, and would never want to hurt him. But I hope you can understand how I feel."

"Sure. Talk to you later. Better go have a little chat with Willie. Like most of us, Willie doesn't have a lot of patience. Bye."

Now I feel rotten. But I hope Becky will make him feel better. I'll think of something to make it up to him. Maybe he can go with Dad and me to the zoo, or something.

Chapter Twenty-Four

When I awoke this morning, and looked at the calendar and my expanded waistline, I realized the time is near.

'Tater Tot,' I said, 'Rest up my little friend, for I have a feeling you and I are going to be pretty busy before many more days have passed.' As usual, Tater -Tot didn't reply -- just gave a little kick. We've had quite a bit of activity lately.

Maybe it's silly to talk to a baby that isn't even born yet, but I'll bet most mothers do it. Somehow it helps me to feel not quite so alone. And I think the baby needs to learn the sound of my voice, so it will know who loves it most.

Today we go to visit Dr. Kradel. This will probably be the last time before the big party. Just want to make sure we're well organized and all is well. I probably should ask Becky to take me since it is difficult to get behind the wheel. But I think I'll take a chance one more time. I'm coming straight home afterwards, so there should be no problems.

~ ~ ~ ~ ~ ~ ~ ~ ~ ~ ~ ~ ~

"Good Morning, Favorite Patient. How's it going?"

"Just fine, Dr. Mike. Well, actually, I'm tired and my back hurts, and my feet are swollen, and I don't want to be pregnant any more."

The doctor laughs -- "A little late to be thinking about that. But maybe you won't have to wait much longer. Let's check you out and see how things are going."

After the examination and I am dressed, the doctor returns but doesn't look very cheerful, and a cold chill runs up my spine. What's wrong? Everything has been going so well.

"Everything looks good," he says. "All the tests give us the right answers. It looks like you may have another week or two, but I don't expect to see you in this office again before delivery."

"That's good news, Doctor. I am very tired. I guess they will call you from the hospital when I get there."

"You're right. Now don't worry. Everything has been normal this far and there's no reason to expect anything else at delivery. I'm glad to see you in such good spirits."

"Yes, I've finally begun to accept reality. I'll be all right. And my Dad will be here for a few weeks. So that will help. But I have a feeling something's troubling you, Doctor. Your whole attitude has changed since I came in."

"I'm sorry. I tried to not let my concern show. My wife has been having more serious problems lately and has come into the hospital. I'll walk out with you and go check on her. I'm sorry, Mrs. Graham. I shouldn't let my personal feelings get in the way. I'll take good care of you when the time comes for your delivery."

"I have no doubt of that. I hope you will find your wife improving, and that she will soon be able to go back home."

"Thank you. See you in a few days."

~ ~ ~ ~ ~ ~ ~ ~ ~ ~ ~ ~

Upon reaching home, I find I have another letter from Mr. Brown, the attorney who is handling Chuck's trust account. It seems to be just a formal reminder that he needs the baby's name and birth certificate before he can complete the changes to the original agreement. He also wishes me well. Some day, maybe this will seem important, but for now, it is the least of my concerns.

~ ~ ~ ~ ~ ~ ~ ~ ~ ~ ~ ~

At last -- this is the day Dad is coming. It will be so good to see him again. I didn't realize how hard it would be to have no one to lean on. I should have called him long ago.

After making sure the house is in order and the preparations for a light supper are taken care of, I sit down to read and relax.

I must have fallen asleep, for suddenly I am awakened by a knock on the door, and look up to see Dad standing there. Quickly I let him in and get one of his good, bear hugs. Then he brings in his things and we put them in the guest room.

"Well," he says, "let me look at you. You are just as beautiful as ever, but a little big around the middle."

"Okay, no funny remarks. I'm aware of my situation."

Then Dad's face sobers, "Are you all right? Everything in order?"

"I'm fine, Dad. I have a great doctor. I wish you could meet him. He inspires confidence. The only thing is, he keeps bringing God into the conversation as he talks about my pregnancy. Reminds me of you."

"Sounds like a fine fellow. Now let's sit down so you can bring me up to date on everything. I can't believe you've gone through all this and never told me. Why? I don't understand."

"You know I've always tried to be so independent, especially ever since God let me down by taking Mother. Oh, how I've wished for her so many times. Losing her was so painful. And she is still needed."

"Yes, I know. It is the hardest thing I have ever had to face."

Suddenly, it hit me -- like a blow to my head. Dad had suffered a great loss, too. But I never had given a thought to his feelings.

"Oh, Dad. I'm so sorry. I have been thinking only of myself. I lost my mother. But you lost your wife -- your other half. I guess losing Chuck gives me an idea of your feelings. How did you put up with me and my selfishness?"

"You are my child. And I love you. I knew you were hurting. So I couldn't blame you for that."

"I'm so sorry, Dad. But when this baby gets here, things will be different. You'll see."

"I'm just thankful that you are well and that you are going to let me be a part of your life again."

Chapter Twenty-Five

In the cool of the evening, we went out to sit on the bench under the maple tree, just to take in the sights and sounds, and relax.

Dad was commenting on what a nice part of town I lived in -- convenient, yet out of the hustle and bustle of traffic and commerce. I was just sitting there soaking up the quiet, and then I felt a wave of contentment sweep over me. It was so unusual; it almost took my breath away. It had been a long time since I felt so at peace.

Just then Willie and Jean magically appeared, coming up the driveway. They greeted us with big smiles and said, "What-cha doing?"

"Oh, nothing. And it feels good," I said. " Jean, I don't believe you've met my father. Dad, this is Jean, Willie's little sister."

My Father smiled and shook her little hand. "Happy to meet you, young lady."

Willie had to get into the act. "Well, Mr. Dobson, she isn't a young lady, but she is a pretty good little sister, most of the time. She needs me to see after her."

"But soon I won't need him," Jean responded. "When I get to be six, I can see after myself."

"Is that a fact? How soon will that be?"

"I don't know. I'll have to ask Willie."

"Well, you are four," said Willie, "so it will take two years for you to get to be six."

"Is that a long time?" Jean wanted to know.

She was looking up at me with the question on her face, so I took that little hand in mine and said. "Well, that depends on how you look at it. It may seem like a long time to you, but when you are older, two years will pass quickly."

"Okay," she said, seeming to have lost interest. Turning again to look at Dad, she said, " We're going too have a baby. Do you know that?"

"Yes, Angela told me."

"Why do you call Missy, 'Angela'?" Jean questioned my Dad.

"Once she was our little baby and that is the name we gave her. Now that she is grown, it seems to me that it fits better than 'Missy.' But you can call her whatever you want, okay?"

"Okay, I'll call her Missy, and I want her to have Tater-Tot right away."

Dad burst out laughing. "Tater-Tot? Is that what you call the baby?"

"That's a good name," spoke up Willie. "You see, we don't know if it's a boy or a girl, so we have to have a name that fits whichever one it is."

"Suits me." And Dad laughed again.

"Willie! Jean! Time for supper," called Becky from her front porch.

The children quickly said good-bye and away they went.

"Great kids," Dad remarked. "They'll keep you company when the baby comes."

"Yes, they really are great kids," I agreed. "And their mother is a special friend. I don't think I would have made it this far, except for Becky."

In a few minutes, we decided to go in and see if we could find something to nibble on for supper. Actually, I was really looking forward to bed time. It would feel so good to stretch out in bed.

~ ~ ~ ~ ~ ~ ~ ~ ~ ~ ~ ~ ~

The bed really felt good and I was asleep almost by the time I could turn out the light.

Then, sometime during the night, a sharp pain jabbed me in the left side of my back. It startled me and I sat up in bed. I felt around on the sheet trying to find what had stuck me. But I found nothing, so I lay back down and began to drift off. Then it hit me again on the right side. Now, I knew something stuck me. I turned on the light and made a thorough search, but found nothing.

'What's going on?' I wondered, as I settled down again, preparing to fall back to sleep. But then, my stomach hurt. I couldn't get comfortable. I looked at the clock. It was 4:30, two and a half hours before I had to get up. I had better settle down and try to rest.

When the next pain hit my body, it also struck my mind, and I realized what was happening. It was time to go to the hospital. I knew there wasn't any hurry, so I took a shower and dressed. Made the bed and made sure I had everything I would need in my overnight case. Then I went in to wake up Dad.

"Dad, I'm sorry to bother you, but I think it is time to go to the hospital." And just as I said that, a pain hit and Dad jumped out of bed. He reached for his trousers. He had a look of panic on his face.

"Take it easy, Dad. You've been through this four times before. This shouldn't bother you."

"I was a lot younger then, remember?" And he dashed around, getting ready to drive me to the hospital.

~ ~ ~ ~ ~ ~ ~ ~ ~ ~ ~ ~ ~

The hospital was quiet just before dawn, and the nurses' soft-soled shoes barely made a whisper as they rushed around getting me into the hospital gown and into bed. Then came the blood pressure check, temperature, etc. and they asked about pains. They began to see several demonstrations of the pains and sent for the head nurse, who took one look and ordered me into the delivery room.

To me, this seemed a little unusual for the first baby to come so soon, but the nurses reassured me that all was well, explaining that the doctor had left orders to give me special care. They didn't want to disappoint him. They told me he would be there in plenty of time, but was presently visiting in his wife's hospital room until he was needed.

They let Dad into my room, briefly. And he sat there looking worried, even though I tried to reassure him.

The nurse began to time my contractions and at a certain point, asked Dad to please go to the waiting room and they would tell him immediately when the baby had arrived. He squeezed my hand and left.

That's when Dr. Mike showed up and gave me a warm, reassuring smile.

"Hello, Favorite Patient," he said. I don't remember when he started calling me that. Maybe he did that for all his patients. But it always gave me reassurance and made me feel like a friend.

He checked me over, and said, "Everything is ready. Let's bring this little one into the world."

I had had just enough medication to make me woozy, yet I was aware of the actual birth and heard the first cry. And my heart gave a jump that even shook the bed.

"A fine boy!" the Doctor said with a smile as the nurse laid him on my tummy.

"Oh, thank you." I guess that remark was for the doctor since I didn't acknowledge God in my life.

"The doctor grinned. Give him a good, strong name," he said. "He'll live up to it."

Just then the nurse tapped him on the shoulder, and he turned suddenly and rushed out the door.

In a few minutes Dad came in. He looked relieved when he saw I was all right -- more than all right. I was the happiest I had been since before Chuck's death.

"Just let me get a look at this young fellow," Dad said, as he reached gingerly to pick up the baby. " Have you thought about a name?" he asked.

"Oh, yes," I exclaimed. His middle name will be Charles for his father, and his first name will be Russell, for his grandfather. "Russell Charles Graham, meet your Granddad."

With tears streaming down his face, Dad looked into the baby's face and said, "May God bless you, my son. Follow Him closely all your life and you will become the man He wants you to be." He closed his eyes, and I thought he must be praying.

Then he handed him back to me, saying, "What a responsibility, my Dear. May God help you."

And for a second, I almost said, "Amen." But then I remembered that I had gotten this far on my own, so I didn't expect God to suddenly take notice of me.

~ ~ ~ ~ ~ ~ ~ ~ ~ ~ ~ ~ ~

When I got home a few days later, the first visitor was Willie, of course.

He rushed right in without knocking, and announced, "I came to see Rusty."

"Whom?" my father asked, with a grin.

Willie was a little impatient. "You know, Rusty, the baby."

"Oh," my father smiled. "Come right this way." And a life-long friendship was begun.

Chapter Twenty-Six

A young man, a Dr. Richter, checked me over before my release from the hospital and I have an appointment with him for my six-weeks' check-up . Seemed a little strange since I had never seen this doctor before, but that may be the way the hospital works.

Now Rusty and I are off to see this 'new' doctor. Rusty seems to be such a happy little fellow who has given very little trouble after the first couple of weeks, when he slept most all day but only certain parts of the night.

Dad stayed for three weeks and believed I had everything under control so he went home to check on things, promising to be back soon.

I was so grateful to him, and the house seemed so empty when he had gone. That's when I began to miss Chuck all over again. 'This baby needs a father,' I said to myself. 'How will he learn all the things Daddies teach their sons? Oh, I plan to do my best, but I know I'm just not qualified to be a parent of any kind, much less a mother and a father.'

We have fun together, Rusty and I, in the mornings at bath time, and often throughout the day as he becomes more alert. But sometimes I would wake up in the middle of the night, so frightened. How could I be sure I was doing the right things for him. What if I didn't teach him right and he turned out to be a drop-out or something worse? Being a mother is such a responsibility. Becky is kind and visits often, but she has her own family to care for. How I wish I had some guidance. Becky seems to be doing a great job with her children. I'll ask her for suggestions about whom to consult the next time we are together.

But right now, we'll check in with this doctor and see what he has to say.

"The Doctor will see you now. It's the third door on the left."

Dr. Richter was standing at his open door expecting us. He greeted me with a warm handshake. And I somehow felt reassured.

"Sit down, Mrs. Graham. And let me have a look at your happy son." Rusty was smiling up at him.

It seems he more often smiles at men than women who coo over him. But that may be just my imagination.

After the nurse measured and weighed Rusty, she brought him back to the Doctor. He took him gently in his hands and looked at him intently, before laying him on the examining table and listening to his heart, lungs and giving him a good check-over.

The Doctor turned to me. "Does he sleep well?" he asked.

"Most of the time," I answered. "Sometimes he does wake up at unusual times during the night. When we get past that two o'clock feeding, I think we'll do better. Why, is something wrong?"

"Oh, no. Quite the contrary. I can tell he eats well. He is a good specimen of a very healthy baby. You can be proud of him and the care you are giving."

I was so pleased, I'm afraid I blushed. "Thank you, Doctor. You don't know how uncertain I feel sometimes, trying to care for him alone, having had no experience."

"I didn't know you were alone. I'm sorry about that. All children need two parents. I'm sure you will agree."

"Most certainly, I do. But my husband was killed in an automobile accident almost a year ago. That should help you understand my grief and uncertainty."

"It certainly does, and makes me admire you more for the care your baby is receiving."

"We will let the nurse care for him a few minutes while I examine you," he said, handing Rusty to the nurse, who seemed glad for the assignment.

After my examination, the Doctor pronounced me fit and having recovered in good condition.

"Don't do a lot of hard labor for a while, but your body has recovered nicely and you will regain your strength quite soon. I don't expect any problems, but if you should need a check-up call Dr. Kradel. He plans to be back in his office soon."

"Thank you. When should I bring Rusty in again?"

" About every four weeks. Dr. Kradel will give you a schedule."

"Dr. Kradel isn't ill, is he? I was expecting him for this check-up."

"I understand. No, he isn't ill. I just supposed you knew. He lost his wife about the time your baby was born. Needed some time off. But should be back soon."

"It's been good to meet you, Mrs. Graham, and your fine young man. Take good care of both of you."

And we were out the door and on our way home -- in shock!

~ ~ ~ ~ ~ ~ ~ ~ ~ ~ ~ ~

I sent Dr. Kradel an appropriate sympathy card, with a brief note explaining that I had just heard about his wife. I expressed my sorrow but I heard nothing from him.

~ ~ ~ ~ ~ ~ ~ ~ ~ ~ ~ ~

My days became fairly routine. Babies have a schedule that takes up most of the morning. But while Rusty napped in the afternoon, I became restless and wanted something productive to do.

More than once I thought about the computer. By this time, they have likely made great strides in development so that they are able to do so many more things than that model Becky and I saw that day of our tour.

I subscribe to a professional magazine. Even though it is difficult for me to read and I get only bits and pieces, here and there, I find the computer mentioned much more often. If I could just see well enough, I might look into getting one for myself.

While thinking of my lack of sight, I remember that Dr. Wallace hasn't seen my new baby. So one sunny, comparatively warm afternoon, I decide to take Rusty for a brief visit.

~ ~ ~ ~ ~ ~ ~ ~ ~ ~ ~ ~

"Hello, Peggy."

"Why, Mrs. Graham, hello. My, you are looking petty today. Are you all right? Is there a problem?"

"No, no problems. I was in the neighborhood and wanted to show off my new son. If Doctor Wallace isn't too busy -- I'll only take a few minutes."

"Oh, yes. Let me see that young man. A handsome fellow. What's his name?"

"Miss Peggy, please meet Russell Charles Graham. Actually he is known to his friends as 'Rusty'."

"Well, I'm very proud to meet you, Rusty. Let me check on the doctor. His next patient is scheduled in about twenty minutes, but I think he is in his office. Be right back."

Miss Peggy is one of the most efficient receptionists in the Eye Clinic. She has become a friend during the time I have been visiting Dr. Wallace. Always has a cheerful word.

"Yes, Mrs. Graham. Come on back. The doctor is free now."

Doctor Wallace was sitting at his desk, looking expectantly at the door as we entered. Immediately he rose, came around to shake hands and take a peek at Rusty.

"And who, may I ask, is this fine fellow?"

"Dr. Wallace, I want you to meet my son, Russell Charles Graham. Oh, he has fallen back asleep. I wanted you to see his eyes."

"I'm glad to meet you, young man, asleep or awake. He looks like a husky fellow. Probably be a football player when he grows up."

"Oh, I hope not. I would be on pins and needles during every game. But I guess we'll just have to wait and see what he wants to do with his life." Laughingly, I continued, "So far, he hasn't suggested anything."

"Well, you're right about that. He is the one to decide what he wants to do, or to be. Some parents make the mistake of trying to live their dreams through their children's lives. It's not fair, and it doesn't work."

"Tell me about your children, Doctor. I never realized before that is what parents like to talk about the most."

"We have three children. The last one, Kenneth, is just finishing high school and will be off to college next fall. His mother is just in a stew about his leaving home. Being faced with an empty nest is hard for both of us. But I wouldn't want to hold him back for anything. He is planning to major in Forestry. Of course he has always loved the outdoor life, but this was kind of a surprise to us. He seems confident, though. So we'll see what happens. There are a number of different directions he can go from there."

"Our second child, Lucille, is quite talented musically and is working on becoming a concert pianist. And Earl, our eldest, is working in the field of mechanical engineering as related to aeronautics. So that's our brood."

"They sound wonderful, Doctor. I know you are very proud of each of them. Some day I'll come back and brag about my son."

As I am rising from my chair, he stops me with his hand. "Just a minute. When you mentioned coming back, that reminded me. When is your next appointment?"

"On the fourteenth. About a week and a half, I think."

"Good. I'm sure you will find a baby sitter. Plan to stay a couple of hours. I want to do some extensive testing. There might be good news ahead."

"Oh!" I exclaim. "What kind of good news, Doctor Wallace?"

"Well, that all depends on the results of the testing. You know research is going on daily in the field of Ophthalmology. There have been a few breakthroughs. I'm not promising anything. I just want to check out things. Don't get your hopes up. This is just the beginning."

"Well, one has to hope, Doctor."

"Yes I know. There's my buzzer. My patient is here. We'll talk about this later."

We shake hands. "See you in a couple of weeks."

He goes to his appointment. I pick up Rusty and "float" home. What if --? But maybe not. Just have to wait and see.

~ ~ ~ ~ ~ ~ ~ ~ ~ ~ ~ ~ ~

I pick up the phone and dial. "Hi, Becky. Can you and Jean come for lunch? It's just soup and sandwich. Of course, Rusty is having strained oatmeal and carrots."

"We would love to," replied Becky. "What time do you want us to come over?"

"Oh, come any time. I'll be putting lunch on the table, so just come on in to the kitchen. Okay -- bye."

Becky and Jean show up shortly and we sit down to eat and visit. Jean is more interested in watching Rusty smear his food on his face and to try to get out of his chair, than in her lunch.

Becky and I discuss this and that -- even the weather. We re just two good friends, relaxing and enjoying being together.

Suddenly Jean spoke up, almost in a panic. She was eyeing Rusty. "How will you ever get him clean again? He has oatmeal and carrots all over everything he could touch, even his hair."

"Don't worry," I laugh. "He's washable. A nice, warm wet wash cloth will shine him up right away. He'll be practically as good as new."

I could see she was a little doubtful, so the first thing I did when we finished eating, was to give Rusty the clean-up treatment and put him in his play pen in the living room. Jean was right there to see after him, and play with him.

As Becky and I cleaned up the kitchen, she asked, "What's up? You seem to have something on your mind."

"I'm trying to not let myself get too excited. After all, he didn't promise anything. But I took Rusty in so Dr Wallace could see him. Wasn't a real appointment. Just a spur of the moment kind of thing."

"But I do have a regular appointment in a couple of weeks and he asked me to get a baby sitter, and plan to be there for a couple of hours or so. Wants to do some extensive testing. He didn't give me any details, but I have a feeling that he plans to try one of the new techniques that research has been developing. So I can't help thinking, wouldn't it be wonderful if I could see again?"

"Oh, Angela," Becky hugged me. "It would be wonderful. We'll pray about it. I'll ask the ladies of the Church Circle to pray, too."

"Whoa -- just a minute! I don't know, for sure, that's why he is testing. I'm just hoping. And we don't need to tell the whole community. They don't really care, anyway."

"Of course, they care. And a little extra praying never hurts. God has His hand on you, Angela. I wish you could see that. He has plans for you. I have no idea what He has in store, but I've felt you were special ever since we first met."

"Oh, Becky -- that's just your kind and generous heart talking. You are the special one. Look what you've done for me. You are my best friend. My only friend, really."

"Well, we sure could fix that quickly, if you would come to church and get acquainted with all the good women there. Each of them would be your friend. We have the 'cream of the crop' in our fellowship."

"Please, Becky. You know how I feel about that. I'm doing fine on my own. I've made it this far without God, so I have reason to believe I can handle things."

Becky shook her head sadly, put her arms around me, then stood back.

"We'd better go," she said. "I know Rusty needs his nap and he won't give up as long as Jean will play with him. Thanks for the lunch. I'll be praying about your visit to Dr. Wallace."

After Becky and Jean left, I put Rusty down for his nap and stood looking at him for a long time as he slept. Of course, I could see him, but it would be wonderful if I had better sight as I looked at him and looked out for him. I needed to be doing some practical things to insure his future.

Ah -- for some reason that made me think of Mr. Brown, the attorney. Then I remembered that I was supposed to send him a copy of Rusty's birth certificate. I had better get it ready to go out in tomorrow's mail.

Chapter Twenty-Seven

As I sort the morning laundry, the phone rings. That's a surprise. Who could be calling at this hour?

"Hello."

"Hello, Angela. This is Doris. How is everything?"

"Fine. How about with you?"

"Great. Say, listen. Your sister-in-law, Betty, and I are thinking about coming to the city to do a little shopping and we would like to see our new nephew. Could you put us up for a night?"

"I -- uh, of course." I didn't hesitate because I didn't want them to come. I was just so surprised that they wanted to. "When will you be here?"

"We thought we would start early in the morning, and get to your place about ten or eleven. We could shop in the afternoon, and finish up the next morning on our way home. Does that sound all right to you?"

"Sounds fine to me. I'll have lunch ready when you get here. Then after Rusty's afternoon nap, we'll meet you somewhere and have a little time together."

"Good idea. We'll make it by eleven, for sure. Thought we might get in a little early Christmas shopping. Neither of us has been to the City for some time. See you tomorrow."

As she hangs up, I stand there holding the phone, puzzled. Of course I'll be glad to see them and make it more convenient for them to do their shopping. But we've had so little contact for the last seven years, I can't help but wonder, why now?

Better do the laundry and make sure the house is in order. Since they know I have trouble seeing, I'll bet they will be checking my housekeeping skills.

For lunch, I'll serve a jell-o salad and chicken salad sandwiches. I'd better borrow Becky's brownie recipe. Her brownies were so good.

~ ~ ~ ~ ~ ~ ~ ~ ~ ~ ~ ~ ~

At about 10:30, I began looking for the girls, and they showed up about fifteen or twenty minutes later.

We did a lot of "Hello's" and hugging, and were so glad to see each other. Then I brought out Rusty for inspection. Just as expected, they agreed that he was perfect. And he rewarded them with a big, wide grin.

That grin looked so much like Chuck, I felt a band tighten around my heart.

"I know you want to get right at that shopping, so come on in to the kitchen. Lunch is ready."

"We better wash up first; maybe bring in our luggage?"

"Sure, Okay. Let me help you. I'm putting you in the back bedroom. Hope you don't mind sharing."

"That will be fine with us. Let us at that food."

It was such a simple lunch, yet they acted like it was prepared by a famous chef. I have the strangest feeling that there is more to this visit than shopping.

When we finished and I began to clear the table, they both rushed to offer help. "Oh, there's not much to do. You go ahead and get started on your shopping. Where shall Rusty and I meet you?"

"Actually, we don't know our way around very well, so maybe we should just wait while Rusty naps, then all go together." This from Doris.

I looked at her with a question on my face, but she didn't say anything more. "Okay, make yourselves at home and I'll go freshen up and be ready when Rusty wakes up."

What were they up to?

~ ~ ~ ~ ~ ~ ~ ~ ~ ~ ~ ~ ~

Our first stop was a big shopping mall, not far from the house. As expected, they were not shopping for anything in particular. They just wanted to look. Doris found a purse she liked, and Betty a pair of shoes. Then they suggested that we stop at one of those little shops and have a dish of ice cream.

When we were settled and had given our order, I checked on Rusty, who seemed to be quietly enjoying himself with all the sights and noises.

"Ok, girls." I couldn't wait any longer. "What's up? There's something funny going on here and curiosity is eating me up. You didn't come all this way for just a purse and a pair of shoes."

They looked at each other as if to say, 'You go first.'

"I'm waiting," I said, tapping my fingers on the table.

Finally Doris spoke. "Well, several things, Angela. We feel we've neglected you through all this. Of course, we didn't know about part of it, but we could have been more supportive after Chuck's death. We're both ashamed of that."

"Yes, we are," Betty cut in. "We excused ourselves by saying you hadn't needed us in the past, so why would you need us now?"

"I understand. Perhaps it was better this way. I was not in any mood to make up for lost time. I felt pretty independent and knew I could handle it. But I had no idea what I was facing. Then things began to stack up and I felt completely alone. That's when I finally weakened and asked Dad to come. He is a real rock, as you know."

"Yes, he is, and we all love him dearly and want him to be happy. But something does kind of bother us. That's why we needed to talk to you."

By this time the ice cream was gone, and we gathered up our packages to make our way back to the car.

"All right, girls. We're all tired, especially Rusty. Lets stop at the grocery store and get a frozen pizza and some salad stuff, and go home. We can kick off our shoes and get comfortable. When we feel like supper, it won't take long. But we can spend the rest of the afternoon with you giving me details of the problem, and me giving you the answers. Okay?"

"Sounds like a good deal," they agreed in unison.

~ ~ ~ ~ ~ ~ ~ ~ ~ ~ ~ ~ ~

Rusty was happy to get back to his play pen. We went to the patio and sat around in our stocking feet. No one said anything. I waited.

"Well?" I prompted.

"Well," Doris finally said, "We think Dad is considering marrying again. There! I've said it out loud!"

I guess I looked a little strange, so Betty spoke up, "He and Lucy Gardner who lives next door, are spending a lot of time together."

I couldn't help it. I burst out laughing.

"It's not all that funny," Doris said. "Why, she's an old woman, probably almost as old as Dad. She'll get sick, and he will have to take care of her, and spend all his retirement money for doctors, and -- you know she has two boys, so no telling what they will want Dad to do. You'd better take this seriously."

"Yes, we've got to put a stop to this before it gets out of hand," said Betty.

I realized they were serious -- really concerned. But I didn't understand why this was a cause for alarm. If Dad wanted to get married, he was a grown man and was old enough to know his own mind.

"All right, girls. I don't really see a problem here, but I'll talk to Dad about it and see what he is thinking. I don't promise anything. But just let me talk with him before you jump in and stir things up. I'm hoping he will be spending a few days with me during the next couple of weeks. I'll check into it and I'll call and let you know. Will that work for you?"

Yes, they agreed.

"I feel better already," Betty said.

"Me, too," from Doris. "Angela could always twist Dad around her little finger," she mused.

So without any more shopping, the girls went back home the next morning, counting on me to talk Dad out of getting married, which wasn't what I had in mind, at all.

Chapter Twenty-Eight

That evening, after I had Rusty bedded down for the night, I called Dad.

"Hello."

"Hello to you. Dad, this is Angela. Just checking in to see if I could get a visit from you. I'm going to need a baby sitter."

"Well, that sounds like a pretty good offer to me. When do you need me?"

"I have an appointment with Dr. Wallace on the fourteenth -- Wednesday. Can you work that in?"

"Yes, that will be fine with me. I'll come on Monday morning and we can have a little visiting-time before hand."

So it was all set. I was eager to learn what the doctor had to say. Somehow, I felt it might be good news. I set about putting the house in order, doing some "fix-ahead" meals to go in the freezer, so I wouldn't have to spend a lot of time in the kitchen while Dad was here.

Rusty was growing by leaps and bounds. He could almost stand alone now, and I knew he would soon be walking . Dr. Mike brags on him every time I take him in. He always wants to hold him and talk to him. In a way, it seems a little strange, but it is probably because he has never had children of his own. And Rusty really thrives on that attention from a man. Oh, how I wish Chuck were here to see his son grow.... and throw in a little help, now and then. Rusty really needs a man in his life. But Dad will be here in a few days and they are always good together.

~ ~ ~ ~ ~ ~ ~ ~ ~ ~ ~ ~ ~

The morning came when I began looking for Dad to arrive. I tried to explain it to Rusty and maybe he got the idea, because he kept saying "Paw-Paw."

He knew only a few words, but I knew the day would soon come when he would begin asking a lot of questions. Sure hope I am wise enough to give him the right answers. I have so many doubts about rearing a boy alone. Of course, I know what Dad would say -- 'Just ask the Lord to help you and trust His direction.' But the Lord is Dad's answer for everything. And it's just not that simple.

Ah --, there's his car in the drive. I grab up Rusty and dash out the door. It's so good to see him.

Dad puts his arms around both of us and gives us a big hug. Then we take his suitcase into the house and settle in the kitchen where I give him a cold drink and Rusty demands one, too.

During the afternoon, while Rusty is napping, Dad and I relax in the living room and catch up on a lot of visiting.

Now seemed like a good time to spring the big question.

"Well, Dad," I begin, "What's this I hear abut you and Lucy Gardner?"

He looked up with a funny expression on his face. "I don't know," he said. "What do you hear?"

"You remember I had company last week, Doris and Betty Jean. Said they wanted to go shopping. But it turned out that they wanted to talk to me about you. They sounded really worried." I couldn't keep from smiling as I spoke.

Dad gave me an uncertain look. "I don't understand why the girls are worried. Lucy and I get along fine. Always have."

"That's the problem. They think you and Lucy are about to get married, and they are concerned about that."

"Get married?" Dad gave a big laugh.

"That was my reaction, too. But I promised them I would talk to you about it."

"Well, it's a ridiculous idea, of course. The Gardner's have been our good neighbors for many years. When your Mother and Bill were alive, both of us couples did a number of good things together. Since they've been gone, Lucy and I are still friends and help each other out from time to time. But there's noting romantic about it. We're just good friends and neighbors, that's all."

"What I don't understand is why they are so concerned. Lucy is a fine woman, and if I decided to get married, that would be my business." Dad was getting a little steamed now. "But the truth is, I've never given remarriage a thought. Your Mother and I had a very special bond and I could never feel that way about anyone else. And marriage without love is not marriage. So you just tell your sister and sister-in-law they have nothing to worry about. If I change my mind, I'll let them know, but I'll not ask their permission!"

"Okay, Dad. Take it easy. I thought it was a joke at first. I'm not sure why it worried them so much, but they were afraid you would have to take care of Lucy in her old age, or something like that. And I understand exactly how you feel. I could never marry again, either. Chuck and I were not married very long, but we were so in love and had the perfect marriage. I would never take a chance on that again."

"Now, not so fast, young lady . I know you aren't ready for marriage right now. But you are young, and you have a son who needs a father. So don't be so positive that God doesn't have something special planned for your future."

I was shocked! How could Dad say that to me? And he always brings God into everything. Doesn't he realize yet that I've done fine without his God and I don't expect that to change. I turned away with tears in my eyes. Dad just didn't understand.

Suddenly I felt his strong arms about me. "There, there, Angela. I'm sorry I didn't mean to upset you. I just believed you hadn't thought that far ahead yet. Don't worry. It will work out for the best. When we trust the Lord, things always do."

I tried to understand. That is just the way Dad is. I settled back in my chair and tried to pull myself together. When I heard Rusty moving around in his crib, I got him up, changed him and brought him to his Grandfather for a play time. Then I went to the kitchen to see what I needed to do about supper, and to put my thoughts back together.

~ ~ ~ ~ ~ ~ ~ ~ ~ ~ ~ ~

The waiting room at Dr. Wallace's office was quiet -- a man, reading a newspaper, and a woman, staring off into space. I went to the counter to check in.

"Good Afternoon, Mrs. Graham," I was greeted. "The Doctor will be ready to see you shortly. Please be seated and I will call you."

A few minutes later, I was shown into Dr. Wallace's office, where he was seated behind his desk. He rose, extended his hand for a shake and asked me to sit.

"Mrs. Graham, we need to talk a little about what I'm considering for your treatment. I want to make sure you feel free to reject this plan if you want to. It's not a requirement. In fact, I'm not sure of the results. If I were, I would be more positive about asking you to do it. However, it has apparently been successful for a number of other patients who have tried it in the last few months. New ideas, treatments, and medications are being discovered and perfected all the time. So we keep trying to find what will be of benefit to our patients."

"What I'd like to do today is give you a series of tests to make sure you are a good candidate for this new procedure. If it appears that you are, I should like to begin the treatment next week."

"Simply put, I will give you a series of three injections in your eye, and hope they will stop the degeneration before it can progress further. If it should prove successful for your better eye, we would eventually want to treat the other. You must understand this will not restore the sight you have already lost. But if it is successful, it will prevent further loss."

I sat quietly, trying to take in all he was saying, but it was a bit confusing. The part I really understood was that if it worked, my sight would remain as it is today. It didn't take long for me to figure out that, until something better comes along, this is the best opportunity to save my sight. I was handicapped with the present loss, but I was still able to do many things that I had expected to lose over time.

"This sounds great to me, Doctor. What do you want me to do?"

"First, the nurse will dilate both eyes with the usual drops. After they have taken effect, she will inject dye into your arm and in a short time, she will be ready to photograph your eyes in a special way that will give us the information we need to make this decision. These photographs will be stored in the computer to give us a more accurate reading, and remain for comparison with future examinations."

And so the fun began. I sat where I was told, opened my eyes or closed them, as instructed. I received the dye, and after a waiting period, sat with my head immobilized as the nurse shot film after film for each eye. It's a good thing my head was braced, because I couldn't help jerking when the fireworks exploded in each eye.

Finally we were finished. The nurse took me to a small sitting room and offered me coffee, tea, or coke. I accepted the coke. "Rest a while," she instructed. "The Doctor will get back to you soon."

About half an hour later, Dr. Wallace came into the room and sat beside me on the couch. There was a smile on his face.

"Good news," he said. "You look like a perfect candidate for the new procedure. Shall we make a date for next Wednesday morning at ten o'clock?"

"That will be fine, Doctor," I said, with a smile on my face and hope in my heart.

~ ~ ~ ~ ~ ~ ~ ~ ~ ~ ~ ~ ~

Becky drove me to the doctor's office for the first injection, which turned out not to be that bad, at all. Actually, I was surprised. To just imagine sticking a needle in your eye sounded horrible, but there was no pain. This doctor knew what he was doing.

The second and third injections were scheduled for the following month, and the month after. Then we might begin to know how we were doing. Now I had no fear. I was looking forward to a more stable life.

Chapter Twenty-Nine

Dad went home a few days after the treatment, promising to come back to baby sit during the next treatments.

As it turned out, however, he was not able to come, so Becky drove me to the doctor's office and kept an eye on Rusty while I was busy. Jean was with us, too. So Becky had help.

Knowing I wouldn't be able to see much for a while, Becky suggested we stop at the park on the way home and let the kids play on the swings. Sounded good. The fresh air would be good for all of us and Becky and I hadn't had a good talk session for some time.

"I really appreciate your giving me your day, Becky. I could never have managed alone. You are my best friend -- my only friend, actually."

"I enjoy your friendship, too. But you need more than one friend. And if you will just come to church with me, I'll introduce you to a number of good people who would love to be your friends."

"Now, Becky -- you have encouraged this before but you know I'm not interested in church. Church people and I would have nothing in common."

"Well, I don't know about that. I'm 'church people' and we get along great."

"But you are special. So don't try to make me feel guilty because I'm not going to church and taking Rusty."

"Oh, so that's what you are feeling guilty about. I'll admit there's a difference in making a decision about your own life, and making one for your child who doesn't even know there is a decision to make. Maybe we could fix that. Rusty is big enough now to be in the preschool class. We could just take him with us and he would listen and learn, and one day, be able to make his own decision. We'll take good care of him. You know how special he is to Willie."

"This way all you have to do is get him ready each Sunday morning, and we'll pick him up. Then, your conscience will be clear, and it will be good for him."

This was something for me to think about. It's true that it had bothered me that he might grow up to be 'a little heathen.' Maybe this was the answer.

"Okay, my friend. We might try it a few weeks. If either one of us changes her mind, no hard feelings?"

"Sounds good to me. When is his next appointment with Dr. Kradel?"

"Oh, that's about a month away, And those check-ups really don't amount anything. Rusty is as healthy as a horse. Dr. Mike keeps making appointments as an excuse to spend some time with Rusty. It's a little strange. But there seems to be a special bond between them."

"Of course Rusty loves the attention and he misses a man in his life, even if he doesn't know it. It's so apparent whenever Dad is here, or he sees Dr Mike, or some other man takes notice of him. I suppose it is only natural. Oh, how I wish Chuck had lived to see his son. They would have been a great pair. I guess I'll always miss him."

"Well, that might explain Rusty's attachment to the doctor. But that doctor has surely delivered hundreds of little boys before."

"That's true and I've thought about that. You know he and his wife never had children and they both wanted them so much. Somehow, I think, that in the doctor's mind, and he doesn't realize it, there is some connection between him and my son because he delivered Rusty the same night his wife died. It's almost as if Rusty were a gift to take her place. Sounds weird, doesn't it?"

"Oh, I don't know. But if he is a good influence on Rusty. I guess no harm's done."

~ ~ ~ ~ ~ ~ ~ ~ ~ ~ ~ ~

I've been reading about computers and seeing them on TV. They are beginning to sound interesting. Now that I have some hope about my eyes, I'm beginning to wonder if I shouldn't consider one and what it could do for me.

So I checked an address of an office supply store, and put Rusty in his stroller and went to see what I could learn.

It was over whelming. I wandered along the aisles looking at the different models. According to the prices, I assumed one was better than another.

And there were stacks of different programs to be added to the computers depending on what you wanted to do with one.

Just as I was about to give up in despair, I was approached by a young man asking if he could help.

"Oh, yes, please. I know absolutely nothing about computers and I'm not planning to buy one today. How does one know what she wants?"

"I would suggest you buy a good, all-purpose machine and learn to use it well, he replied. Later you can buy additional programs to fit your particular interests."

"Thank you. That makes good sense. Do you have instructors here?"

"Sorry. We don't. Computer people are pretty independent. Let me check in the office. They might have a suggestion."

He returned in a few minutes. Here are the names of a couple of guys who are real computer whizzes. One of them might work with you in his spare time."

"Thank you so much. Perhaps it would be wise to talk with one of the individuals you mentioned, and let him advise me what to buy. Thank you for your time and trouble."

As we left the store, I mulled all this information over in my mind. I wasn't really ready to make a serious start with computers yet. But they were interesting and I wanted to learn more about them.

But I didn't make it home that day. As I stepped off the curb, pushing the stroller, I turned my ankle and fell. The stroller rolled right on, out into traffic.

Before I could get to my feet, cars began honking, and brakes were squealing, and people were yelling.

One woman ran after the stroller and brought Rusty back safely. And another tried to help me to my feet, but the ankle was too painful. I couldn't stand.

Then she asked if there were someone she could call. Of course, the only person I could ask for help was Becky.

She showed up shortly, taking Rusty in tow, and insisting on taking me to the emergency room.

"It's only a sprain, I assured her. It will be all right in a couple of days."

But she didn't listen. Just drove on as if I hadn't said anything. And afterwards I was thankful.

There was a broken bone that had to be set and put in a cast. I was embarrassed as well as in pain. The nurse informed me that I would be staying in the hospital overnight, so they could check on the ankle, now and then. to make sure it was reacting properly.

Becky took Rusty home with her, and I spent a restless night. The nurses awakened me every couple of hours, or so, to check my ankle.

The next morning, they declared me fit to go home, but outfitted me with a crutch. I felt ridiculous!! And all thoughts of computers left my mind as I recuperated.

Chapter Thirty

All my life, I've heard people complain about the speed of time. Someone was always saying, "It can't be Thursday already." "How did this happen? Only yesterday I left home, and now I have three kids." "Christmas, again? We just had Christmas."

But I never had that problem. Time moved smoothly for me. I had things in hand and they moved in an orderly fashion. That is, they did, until the day I looked at the calendar and realized that, in three weeks, Rusty would start to Kindergarten. Impossible! How could five years pass so quickly? I couldn't let my baby go out into the world alone. He was only five years old!

I tried to think of a way I could keep him home another year. But he had been fully indoctrinated by Willie and was so excited about going to school, he really didn't want to think of anything else.

The day came, and I put my heart in my pocket and prepared to go.

"You don't have to go with me, Mommy. I'll just go with Willie and Jean, and the other kids."

"Yes, Dear, I do have to go -- the first day, anyway. I need to meet your teacher and see your school."

"But, Mommy. You've seen the school lots of times. We drive right by it when we go to the store."

"I know, Honey, but this is different. Some day you will understand. Tomorrow, you can walk to school with the others."

~ ~ ~ ~ ~ ~ ~ ~ ~ ~ ~ ~ ~

Now, I knew it was true -- time does pass quickly. Dr. Wallace has continued the injection treatment to both eyes by now and has me to come into the office every three months for a check-up. So far, I'm doing well. No, I don't see as perfectly as I once did, but I see so much better than I had expected to see by this time. I am very fortunate.

These thoughts bring me to the realization that I need to be doing something worthwhile with my time, now that Rusty will be away most of the day.

The phone rings, and I'm startled to hear Mr. Brown, the lawyer, say, "Mrs. Graham? Good morning. I now have all the papers set up for the Trusts. Up until this time, we have been operating under Mr. Graham's earlier instructions, but the time has come to give an accounting and get your signature on all the forms. Would it be convenient for you to come in one morning this week?"

"Yes, of course. What day would you prefer?"

"Thursday at ten, if that will work into your schedule."

"That will be fine. I'll see you then."

~ ~ ~ ~ ~ ~ ~ ~ ~ ~ ~ ~ ~

When I entered his office, Mr. Brown offered me a chair beside his desk, which was almost covered with legal-looking papers.

"As we begin," he said, I need to explain the capital to you. Some is in real estate -- this varies from time to time as we buy and sell. We have diversified the cash investments -- Government and Municipal Bonds, and the Stock Market. These are more liquid assets and require more overseeing. Our fee is calculated at the end of each calendar year as we appraise the increase in value of the holdings. We receive twenty percent of the increase. This, of course, keeps us on our toes. The larger the increase, the greater the fee we earn."

"Now, according to Mr. Graham's instructions, I have divided the assets into two accounts of comparable value. One-half was to go to his wife, and the other half to his children. I trust this is agreeable to you?"

"Yes, I believe that is what Chuck wanted to do -- leave his family provided for. Since we don't have any urgent needs right now, will you be able to continue caring for the funds as you have in the past?"

"Yes, of course. It was on that assumption that I have drawn up these papers for you to sign for yourself and as guardian for your son."

I signed the papers without reading them. I know that isn't wise, but Chuck trusted this man and his firm, so I will, too.

After shuffling the papers and placing the ones I had signed in a separate stack, Mr. Brown said, "Now for the accounting. These are the figures from the beginning of this calendar year, plus the transactions since then, less our estimated fee. These are for your files."

He handed me two identical lists, one with my name on it, and the other with my son. I took a quick glance at the 'bottom line'.

"Mr. Brown, I don't understand. Surely you don't mean that each of us owns assets valued at this amount?"

"Yes, of course. We have been taking care of thee funds for some time and have made some fortunate investments. I hope you are pleased with the results."

"Mr. Brown, I guess you could say I'm pleased, but astonished is more like it. I had no idea. Of course Rusty's share will ensure his education, but it frightens me to be responsible for the wise use of that much money."

"I understand it must be more than you expected. But you are a wise, young woman, and the Lord will guide you in making the right decisions."

"No, Mr. Brown. You don't understand. The Lord has nothing to do with my decisions. I have done quite well on my own for several years, now. I shall work this out in time. Thank you, so much, for your help. You have been a good steward and I continue to trust you as Chuck did."

We shook hands, and I left, my head reeling with the thought of all that money. One thing, I knew for sure, it wouldn't make any difference in the way we were living now. There just wouldn't be any worries about Rusty's education."

~ ~ ~ ~ ~ ~ ~ ~ ~ ~ ~ ~ ~

One day, shortly after Rusty started school, he came home just bursting to show me something, "Mommy, Mommy, just look! I can draw!"

I took the paper he had extended to me, but really couldn't make much of it. "Where are your glasses, Mommy? Can't you see? It's a house."

I still couldn't see a house. "Sorry, Son. Where are the walls? Where is the roof? I must be looking at it wrong."

"Yes, Mommy, you are. This house isn't built yet. This is a picture showing where the rooms are going to be. I saw the men at the new house on the corner looking at a paper and I asked them what the paper was for. They told me it showed them where and how to build the house. Then they showed me a picture of what the house was supposed to look like when it is finished. So I played like I was building a house and drew the plans."

I was surprised, to say the least. On second look, it did resemble a floor plan.

"That's wonderful, Honey," I said. "You are really pretty good."

"Oh, I don't know anything yet, but I will study, and one day I will build houses, and buildings, and hospitals, and schools, and --"

"Wow! That's a big order. Let's take it slow, okay?"

But, as I thought about it, I realized his dream might come true. Both his parents were artists, of a sort. So why not?

~ ~ ~ ~ ~ ~ ~ ~ ~ ~ ~ ~ ~

"Mommy, when are we going back to see Dr. Mike?"

"Well, I don't know, Honey. We don't have any reason to go. I don't have any problems and neither do you."

"But he told me to come back soon. And this is past 'soon.' It's been a long time. He said I could visit with him while you went shopping, or something. Then I wouldn't be any bother, and we could visit. I like Dr Mike, Mom. He is a nice man and he is good to me."

"I know, Honey. But he is a doctor and a very busy man. He certainly doesn't have time to baby-sit."

"I'm not a baby any more so he wouldn't have to sit. We could talk and stuff. Please, Mom. Let's go see him."

"I'm afraid that isn't a good idea, Son. But I could call him and ask when would be a good time to meet him in the park. Then you two could visit while I run my errands. How about that?"

"Sounds good. I bet we can go any time. Dr. Mike likes me, too."

So that afternoon, I called the Doctor's office. "The Doctor is with a patient right now. May I have him call you back when he is finished?"

"Certainly. Thanks," I replied.

~ ~ ~ ~ ~ ~ ~ ~ ~ ~ ~ ~ ~

"Hello, Mrs. Graham. The nurse said you wanted to speak with me. Is Rusty all right?" It was Dr. Mike Kradel calling.

"Oh, yes. He's fine. A little too much energy, maybe. He insists he needs to see you. He tells me you are great friends and he was supposed to come back to visit you. I'm afraid that he is too 'taken' with you. But you seem to be the main man in his life. I don't want him to become a pest. But I was wondering if you might have an hour or so, some afternoon, and could meet him in he park. I could use the time to run some errands."

"That's a wonderful idea. How about tomorrow afternoon, around three? I don't have any appointments after that. So you could take all the time you need. Tell Rusty to bring his ball and bat. We might get in a little practice."

So Rusty and Dr. Kradel developed a steadfast friendship. It was strange in a way, yet, I suppose, each filled a need for the other.

Rusty also continued going to church with the Rogers family week after week. Often he would come home and tell me some things he had learned. I didn't see any harm in it, so I let it continue.

There soon became a time, each Sunday morning, when I could put everything aside and attempt to sketch again. But it was very frustrating. I had lost so much time and was just "out of practice." The lost sight was a real hindrance.

That was when I began thinking about computers again. I knew there was a program that would enlarge what was on the viewing screen. Maybe that would help me see more clearly.

Rusty was in the fifth grade by this time. Perhaps it was time to look up one of those 'technological gurus' to get some advice and consider buying a computer.

Chapter Thirty-One

The next time Dr. Mike offered to take Rusty for an afternoon together, I used the free time to get back to researching computers.

In one office supply outlet, the clerk was very knowledgeable about different types of computers, and those equipped to do specific things. Although it was easy for him to recognize that I knew absolutely nothing, he seemed to enjoy explaining the different models.

When he learned that my main interest was in clothing design, he took me to an elaborate machine and began to demonstrate. It was fantastic. I could hardly believe it. It was almost as if all I had to do was think of a line of clothing and it would appear on the screen. The price of the computer seemed a little high, but I agreed to think about it.

His brother-in-law, he explained, was an instructor in a nearby high school, but would be available to give me instruction in the late afternoon or evenings. He asked for my telephone number and promised the teacher would call me about an appointment.

Somehow, I felt real good about that. It seemed I now had a purpose, and someone to help to find my way.

Two days later, the young man called, giving his name as James (Jim) Sparks, and asked if he might come over.

After he arrived, we talked, mainly, about computers in general. It was his suggestion that I begin with a well-equipped personal computer and learn as much about it as I could. It would always be useful to me for correspondence and storing information. The main thing was to learn how it operated, and how certain commands caused related things to happen. He said a good general knowledge of computer "language" would benefit me in using a machine designed for a specific purpose.

As we talked, it began to make sense to me and I agreed to purchase a good personal computer and he agreed to teach me all there was to know about it.

Two days later, checkbook in my purse, I arrived at the computer store, prepared to make a purchase.

As I looked about, I was overwhelmed. So many to choose from, and I was so ignorant in knowing what was best.

"Hello, again," said a voice at my elbow.

I turned to find the clerk who had been so helpful the first day. "Jim sent me," I said.

The clerk smiled. "Yes, I know. He said you would be coming in, and for me to steer you in the right direction."

"I'm glad," I said, "for I have no idea what computer would be best for my needs."

"Jim suggested I sell you the latest model at the top of the line. It will not go out of date quickly, and likely may be the only PC you will ever need. After you master it, then we'll get down to business with more technical equipment."

"A good plan," I said. "Point the way."

He didn't hesitate, but took me to a display featuring the top of the line. "It is expensive," he said. "But I can guarantee it will be worth it if you are seriously considering clothing design later on."

So I made my purchase and rushed home to prepare the special place for it. He had agreed to have it delivered that afternoon.

After having the computer placed on its special desk, I sat in the chair and gave it a long, hard look.

'Look, my new friend,' I said. 'You and I have a lot to learn about each other. We are going to work together for a long time, become good friends, and make a name for ourselves.'

When Rusty came home from school, he was so excited. He danced 'round and 'round it. "Can I touch it?"

"Of course you can touch it. It won't break. We just don't know how to use it yet."

But in time, we learned -- both of us. And sometimes I think Rusty learned faster than I did. He could pick up on a lot of things by himself. It seemed he could make it jump through the hoop any time he wanted to. When something went wrong, he could usually get it back on track in a little while.

I was proud of him and his ability, for I believed computers were here to stay and this knowledge would benefit him all his life. Even as computer technology evolved, he would grow along with it.

~ ~ ~ ~ ~ ~ ~ ~ ~ ~ ~ ~ ~

I had been so excited about the new computer that I had forgotten to ask Rusty about his time with Dr. Mike.

When I thought of it later, Rusty gave me a strange look, paused, then said, "Well, -- we had a good time. We always do. But Dr. Mike seemed so sad all day. When I tried to talk to him about it, he just put his arm around me and sat, just looking off into the distance. When I asked him what was wrong, he looked at me, then put his arm around me again and said, 'Rusty, you must know I love you. I wish I had a son like you. But, of course, that'll never happen.' Then he stood up and we began to walk back to the car."

"Oh," I said. "I understand because he is so lonely. I don't know what I would do without you."

"Mom, could we ask Dr. Mike to come over for supper sometime? I think it might make him feel better. I like him, so much, Mom. I guess he is kind of like a Dad to me since mine is gone. Could we ask him to come?"

This took me by surprise and I hesitated. I felt sorry for Dr. Mike, too. I liked him. I thought he was good for Rusty. But I didn't feel ready to ask a man to come to my home for dinner. But after looking at the expression on Rusty's face, I didn't have the heart to say, "No." So I suggested Rusty talk to Dr. Mike about it and see if he were willing, or had the time, and if he were agreeable, it would be all right with me.

I felt safe in passing the buck. Dr. Mike was a busy man and he hadn't been alone as long as I had, so I really didn't think he would accept the invitation. But he did.

A deal was worked out whereby Dr. Mike would meet Rusty at church on Sunday morning and then come home for dinner.

That was not what I expected. But I wanted Rusty to be happy and proud of his home. So I put extra effort into a good "Sunday Dinner" and had the house shinning. Then I sat down to wait for them.

When Rusty and Dr Mike came in, the Doctor shook my hand and began to apologize. "Angela, I'm so sorry. I certainly didn't mean for you to miss church to cook a meal for me."

"Oh, Dr. Mike. I didn't. I thought you knew that I don't go to church. We talked about that long ago."

"Yes, I remember now. But I didn't take it seriously. I thought it was just a passing thing because of your grief. But I'm thankful Rusty attends."

"The neighbors have been very kind to include him in all the church activities. The reports I have are that he behaves himself well."

"Well, of course he does. That's the kind of person he is." Then he fell silent as Rusty came dashing into the room.

Dinner seemed to go over well. We chatted about this and that. But Rusty soon became impatient and dragged the Doctor into the living room to play a board game.

But by the time I had cleared the table and set the kitchen to rights, they were involved in a discussion about books. It turned out, they were both book worms. Rusty was showing some of his favorites, and Dr. Mike promised to lend him a couple that were some of his when he was a boy.

The Doctor thanked me for the dinner, said it was excellent, and expressed his pleasure at being able to spend some time with Rusty in his home.

I wasn't exactly sure how I was supposed to respond, but I thanked him for coming and asked him to come back again.

Chapter Thirty-Two

As to be expected, the more Rusty grew, the more time he spent with Willie. Willie was the big brother Rusty needed to lead him along the way. And he was trustworthy. I never had to fear that Rusty would be led astray.

They played ball. They took walks in the small woods back of the Rogers' house, or fished for minnows in the little stream. As the weather grew cooler, they spent more time indoors, either here or at Willie's house.

They like board games, and, now that both of them were learning a little about the computer, they can spend hours messing with it. Another good thing -- both of them like to read on bad weather days, so they can curl up in front of the fireplace and be happy, especially if I pop corn or make brownies.

This leaves me with some free time to tinker with the computer and I learn more of the things it can do. I can forget about the boys and work in peace.

And apparently they forget about my being just in the next room. I hadn't paid attention to what they were reading, but it must have had something to do with their Sunday School lesson.

I heard Willie say, "Does it bother you that your Mom doesn't go to church?"

There was a quiet pause. "Yeah, some, I guess. Your Mom always goes. Does that make her better?"

"I don't know, but it feels better to me. I think God is taking care of our family because both Dad and Mom believe in Jesus. I believe in Him, too. You remember when I went to camp. What do you think?"

"I don't know much about that stuff. I just like to go, listen to the stories and be with the other kids. There are good kids in Sunday School. Why are you thinking about that?"

"I don't know, but I have to think about it some more," replied Willie.

Then things got quiet again, so they must have returned to their books. But this bothered me. I loved Willie, dearly. But I didn't want him getting Rusty all confused about God. Maybe I should quit letting him go to Sunday School with the Rogers.

~ ~ ~ ~ ~ ~ ~ ~ ~ ~ ~ ~

It was several weeks after that conversation when Rusty came home one Sunday, went in and washed his hands, came and sat at the table for dinner, but didn't say a word. He seemed to be in a deep study.

"What's going on, Buddy?" I asked.

"What?" He looked a little startled. "Oh, nothing. -- May I have some bread, please?"

"Yes, you may. But something's bothering you. Want to tell me about it?"

"Oh, it's nothing. I just don't understand. This morning when the pastor gave the invitation -- you know, when people go up front to get saved or join the church or something, -- well, Willie went up there and he was crying, but his Mom and Dad seemed so happy. I never saw Willie cry before, even when he mashed his finger. And he is the best kid I know. So why did he go up there in the first place? I don't know who to ask. I wish Grandpa were here. He would know. But I know you aren't interested in that stuff so you probably wouldn't know anyway. It just bothers me."

And I sat there with my mouth open, staring at my son, wishing I could help him, but I really didn't know what to say.

As soon as dinner was over, Rusty asked if he could go see Willie. I couldn't think of a good reason to say "No," so I let him go. And I settled down to read a novel I had started a few days ago.

I was thankful for the little reading gadget, called, "Pebble," that I had purchased at Dr. Wallace's suggestion. It made it much more comfortable for me to see the written word, and I had begun to enjoy an old favorite past time, reading.

But in a little while, Rusty was back asking if he could go to church with the Rogers family that evening. Willie was going to be baptized and he wanted to be there. He explained that Willie was saved a few years ago at camp, but never did join the church or was baptized. Willie told Rusty it had bothered him. He didn't know why he waited so long.

Now, I really was at a loss. Should I allow him to go and maybe encourage him to believe in this religious stuff. If I did, and he got disappointed later, as I did, we would both be sorry. Yet if I didn't let him go, I would have to explain, and I didn't know how to do that. So I finally said, "All right."

In the days that followed, Rusty didn't mention Willie's baptizing and I finally decided he had just been curious. But now it was forgotten.

Chapter Thirty-Three

The time to visit Dr. Wallace rolled around again. I was looking forward to his report and to learn what comes next.

As usual, the Doctor was punctual, kind, and in a pleasant mood. We went through the regular routine of the examination. Finally, Doctor Wallace turned to me and said, "Well, my friend, things look pretty good. Tell me what you think."

"I suppose everything is about like it was, especially with my right eye. And I believe that's what you were hoping for. But the left eye seems to be seeing less. Oh, I can still see around the edges pretty well, but if I close my right eye, I can hardly read at all. It's very scary."

"I'm sure it is. So do I have your permission to give it the same treatment we did on the other eye? You realize this treatment will not improve your vision, but we are hoping it will stop the degeneration."

"Yes, of course. I want you to do all you can to help me see. I realize that, even though I cannot see much with the left eye, what I can see helps the right eye. So, I'm ready whenever you are."

The Doctor injected the medication into my eye, and made appointments for the additional two injections that would be needed. Then he reassured me, and told me never to give up. There are a lot of possibilities ahead.

On the way home, I stopped to see the clerk at the computer store, to pick up a printer ribbon and to ask him a few questions about some software I was trying to learn.

"Hey, I'm glad to see you. I have something to show you that I think you might like."

He took me into his office, sat me down in front of a computer, clicked a few things, then stepped back, saying, "Now, how is that? Any better?"

"Oh my!" I exclaimed. "This is wonderful! I can see every word and design perfectly. What did you do?"

"Well, not much. But some wise fellow wrote this program, called "ZOOM." And that's what it does -- makes everything larger and easier to see. Probably you would like to purchase this program. It's not that expensive."

"Not, probably. You knew I would want it as soon as I saw it."

"Good. I had one put back for you and Jim will bring it to your next lesson and install it. There's not much to learn about it and it is simple to use."

~ ~ ~ ~ ~ ~ ~ ~ ~ ~ ~ ~ ~

The Doctor was right. There are great things ahead for me. During my visits with Dr. Wallace, Rusty was spending more time with Dr Mike. Although I was not aware of it at the time, they were having a serious discussion about their relationship.

Rusty was not comfortable addressing his friend as Dr. Mike. It seemed too formal and didn't fit their close connection with one another. He knew the Doctor loved him, and he loved the Doctor in return. Dr. Mike was the most important man in his life. He wanted to grow up to be a man like him and he wanted to call the Doctor, "Dad."

Dr. Mike tried to explain to Rusty that he really wasn't his father, and his mother would surely object to calling him "Dad." Although the boy felt like a son to him, he didn't want to overstep his position or do anything that might interfere with their present, wonderful relationship. The Doctor suggested, "Why don't you just call me, 'Sir.' That's not so formal and no one should object to that. In return, I'll call you, 'Russ.' No one else does that, so it will just be between us."

So Rusty agreed, but he still liked, "Son," much better.

Perhaps if I had known about that discussion, I wouldn't have been quite so surprised when, on my next visit to Dr. Mike's office for my regular check-up that the discussion got around to my calling him "Doctor" Mike.

"You know, Angela, every since you began coming to me years ago, I always called you by your given name, when others aren't around. Yet, after all this time, you persist in calling me "Doctor" Mike. What's wrong with just calling me, 'Mike'?"

"Well, I don't know. You are my doctor -- just habit, I guess."

"I thought we were closer friends than that. Rusty and I worked out the name calling for ourselves because he wasn't happy with calling his best friend, 'Doctor.'"

"I see. Well, we are good friends so I'll try to remember to use just 'Mike'. If I forget, just overlook it. Speaking of friends, you haven't been to supper with us lately. How soon can we fix that?"

"Maybe tomorrow evening, unless something comes up and I have to be at the hospital."

"Good," I said. And we left it at that.

~ ~ ~ ~ ~ ~ ~ ~ ~ ~ ~ ~

But all my life was not spent visiting with doctors. I was eager to get the Zoom program installed on my computer and learn how it would help me.

Of course, I could tell as soon as Jim stepped back from the computer and said, "Let her go!" that everything was so much larger and easier to read. I soon learned it was also adjustable, if I needed larger type. It was wonderful and I began, right away, to practice different things, checking how much easier it was to do the work when I could see it.

In a few days, Jim came carrying a thick notebook, with pictures, diagrams, and explanations.

"Maybe it's time to start thinking about a specific type of computer," he said.

And my heart gave a lurch as I thought it might be possible to design again.

So we looked through his notebook, settled on a model, which he promised to order the next day, directly from the company. "It will take about a week for it to be shipped," he said, "and then we'll see what happens."

What happened was that it wasn't as easy as I had expected it to be. Also, I quickly discovered that I had been left behind in the fashion world. Styles had changed so much. Fewer dresses and skirts were being worn. There were more pant suits and casual wear. Actually, I wasn't pleased with the trend. I thought most of it looked tacky.

So Becky and I made one of our numerous shopping trips just to scout around and see what was going on.

All of the little shops along the downtown streets were full of "junk" and happy, teenaged buyers. I heard so much "Oh-ing and Ah-ing" that it didn't take me long to see all I wanted to.

"After lunch, let's go up on Broadway and Grand, and see what the better shops offer," Becky suggested.

We found a little sandwich shop with a quiet, corner booth and ate our pleasant lunch.

"Tell me about this handsome doctor friend that always meets Rusty at church," Becky said. "They seem very close, and he is a mighty nice-looking man," Becky remarked with a certain gleam in her eye.

"I don't know what you're talking about. Rusty's doctor friend belongs to an uptown church."

"Not any more, he doesn't. About a couple of months ago, he moved his membership to our church and they are always together. He attends other services, too. But when Rusty is there, they sit side by side. And Willie is right beside them. He thinks the doctor is special. How did they meet? And why are they so close? And why haven't you mentioned him to me?"

"Whew! That's a lot of questions. I believe we talked about this once before. The first answer is that Dr. Mike is the doctor who delivered Rusty. It was the same night his wife died. Somehow I think that has created a bond between them. Dr. Mike has no children. So I guess Rusty fills that void for him."

"I didn't know he had moved to your church, but he is good for Rusty, who needs a good man in his life, so I haven't interfered. Now, don't start jumping to conclusions. Mike and I are friends. Nothing more. For one thing, he takes his faith very seriously, and you know how I feel about that."

"Yes, I know," she said, suddenly looking down at her plate. She became very quiet.

When she spoke again, it was to suggest a store we should visit first.

The atmosphere on Broadway was somewhat different from downtown. Even the material used in the garments was of a far better quality. But some of the designs were similar. There were some beautiful dresses and formals. But there was a large array of sport clothes and many attractive pant suits.

It really opened my eyes. I knew I had more to learn than just how to use the computer if I planned to enter the clothing design market again.

We were tired from walking and looking, but we enjoyed our day together. I thanked Becky for her help as we parted at the driveway.

Her parting remark echoed in my head -- "I think you had better think about getting better acquainted with Rusty's doctor."

~ ~ ~ ~ ~ ~ ~ ~ ~ ~ ~ ~ ~

After my shopping trip with Becky, I began to research the new materials now available for clothing construction. Great strides had been made in increasing the durability of some fabrics. Others had the ability to hold creases and be washable without losing shape or color. There were also more decorative materials were available. It wasn't just "buttons and bows" any more.

I visited the large MacMullin House of Fabric which had been the main source of materials for Baker House when I worked there.

I spent one whole afternoon going from table to table, feeling the fabric, admiring the beautiful colors and dreaming of what one could do with this fantastic cloth.

The next afternoon, I went to the library and checked out three volumes on "Clothing Design, Past and Present." Then I spent the rest of the week studying and making notes. I would soon be ready to work with Jim on the new computer.

But all this activity and giving so much thought to design, was often interrupted with visions of Becky telling me about Dr. Mike, the boys and the church. The more I tried to put it out of my mind, the more it haunted me.

I should never have let Rusty get involved in all that church stuff. I felt surrounded by Becky, the boys, and now, Dr. Mike. I was completely caged in as they discussed God and His great love for people.

If I hadn't known better, by my own experience, I might have weakened to their arguments. But I held fast. I was sure, while other people claimed that God loved them, I knew that He didn't love me. He had left me all alone to get by on my own. That was proof enough.

With that settled in my mind again, I went back to the peace and quiet of making plans for the future.

However, all that was quickly side-tracked when Rusty came in from church one Sunday morning, with tears shinning in his big, beautiful brown eyes. It broke my heart to look at him.

But he was so excited, he couldn't stand still . "Oh, Mom," he said as he put his arms around my waist, "I was saved this morning! I was feeling so awful, I knew God was speaking to me, and finally, I just HAD to say to Him, 'Yes, take my life.' And I walked down front and gave my hand to the pastor and told him God had saved me."

He paused for breath. And my heart stood still. I was remembering a similar experience I had many years ago. But so much had happened since then. I couldn't turn back the clock.

And I wasn't so sure I was happy about Rusty's decision. What lay ahead for him? Would he be hurt as I had been? Was that what I wanted for him?

But he wasn't finished. "And, Mom, I'm going to be baptized tonight and I need you to be there."

Oh, I didn't know if I could handle that. "You'll be all right," I said. "You don't need me."

"Of course I do. You are my Mother. Dr. Mike – er, 'Sir,' said he will come by and pick us up in his car and take us to the church. I already told him you would go."

"Well, I guess that settles it, then," I said. But I wasn't happy about it. And I could tell Rusty was disappointed.

That night I went with Rusty and Mike to the church and watched as Rusty was baptized as I had once been.

Now I suppose he will think everything will be perfect from here on out, and I don't have the nerve to tell him differently.

Chapter Thirty-Four

The new computer was so fascinating!! It amazed me the way it took a small command and produced just what I had in my mind.

Jim was an excellent instructor and he and Rusty were great friends. So often I felt Rusty looking over my shoulder as Jim explained the system.

Naturally, I thought he was a very bright boy. After all, he was my son. But I believed he had a special gift for visualizing something, and then knowing how to get it to show up on the screen. We often joked that we needed two computers so we wouldn't get in each other's way.

By the time Rusty was in high school, he began to talk, seriously, about college. He began to study catalogs from different schools to see which one might fit him best. He had no trouble deciding what he wanted to study. That had been plain to him almost from the beginning. He wanted to study architecture. Even in high school, he turned his history lesson into a study of the buildings of that time period. And science class taught him about different materials used in building. Math gave him a chance to learn about calculating dimensions and proportion. He took his "calling" very seriously.

So naturally the subject of money then came up. He had a part-time job and had been saving his money, but it wasn't accumulating very quickly.

This seemed the proper time to tell him that his education was paid for. I explained a little about the financial holdings his father had started years ago, and how they had grown over time, so that there was ample to handle all the education he wanted.

Of course he was pleased, but said that God had inspired his father to start that fund so his children would be taken care of, even if his father were not there. I called it good judgment and planning. But Rusty was certain he was in God's plan, even before he was born. How could I discourage him?

Mike came around more often now and usually, at least once a week, all three of us would go out to eat. Or Mike would think of some place to take us.

We never missed a Builder's Open House whenever one was on display. Rusty always had a field day, examining everything about the place, including all the appliances and fixtures, the different types of wood or other material used. Sometimes I saw him making notes.

I was almost as bad when we attended a fashion show. I was also observing and learning. Many things had changed in the fashion industry during my absence.

Mike was very kind and considerate in taking us to these exhibitions. But he would also take us to boat shows or a picnic at the edge of a nearby lake.

All in all, we had good times together, and without realizing it, we grew closer, almost like a family. Except, of course, on Sunday, when Mike and Rusty went to church and I stayed home and prepared dinner.

Mike often protested this arrangement. He would be glad to take us out. He felt I could use the time much better by being in church. But since I never answered a statement like that, and silence hung heavy in the air, he soon learned not to bring it up. I had the strange feeling, though, that he and Rusty were plotting against me. I'm sure they had a secret agreement to pray for me.

At this time, however, my mind and time were consumed with learning how to sketch on the computer. With the "Zoom" program showing me every detail in large size, and the computer obeying my commands, I began to be able to sketch simple things. It was really thrilling to see designs show up under my fingers again. Of course, I had a lot to learn and I needed practice. But time would help -- if my eyes held out.

~ ~ ~ ~ ~ ~ ~ ~ ~ ~ ~ ~ ~

The nurse called me into Dr Wallace's office and, after greeting and seating me, put drops into my eyes. Then she told me to relax and the doctor would be in shortly.

As I sat and waited, my mind drifted back to the first day I had been there -- so young, so full of grief, so eager to get some glasses and get back to work because I believed it would be my salvation.

Involuntarily, a shiver ran up my back as I remembered the doctor's diagnosis of Macular Deterioration and the fear of blindness that overtook me.

Today, I sat with hope. I had faced reality and realized I would never see as I once did, but the new injections have given me hope that I will never get worse. That is a wonderful comfort which allows me to plan ahead. Suddenly my thoughts were interrupted by the doctor's entrance.

"Hello, young lady," he greeted me. Give me a good word."

"Sunshine," I said.

He chuckled. "That certainly is a good word after all the rain and flooding we've had lately. You are pretty clever. But how about the eyes?"

"They seem the same to me, Doctor. No better, but no worse. So I guess that is the most I can hope for. But I appreciate that."

"How about being a little 'thankful' along with your appreciation?" He smiled.

"All right. If that will make you feel better, I'm thankful. Why does it feel like everyone is ganging up on me about religion lately?"

"Sorry. I didn't mean to upset you. But when I have a successful outcome I realize I didn't do it by myself, and I always thank God. I realize some of my patients do not share my faith, you being one of them. Guess I thought we were good enough friends that I could get by with slipping it in. And maybe God thought you needed a little reminding. Now let's take a look at the eyes and see what they tell us."

I sat quietly as the Doctor carefully studied both eyes. Then he pushed the machine out of the way and smiled.

"Everything is really looking good. I would say both eyes are stable. Of course, as I've told you repeatedly, this research is still in the experiential stage. But I am very encouraged. Let's keep to your regular check-up schedule, at least for a while. If you have any problems, or suspect any change, call or come in so we can find out what's going on."

He stood up and put out his hand to shake mine. "Keep up the good work," he said. "And don't be surprised if God keeps speaking to you through people who care about you." Then he was gone.

I sat in my chair a few minutes thinking of all he had said and what it meant in my life. Finally I gave my head a little shake, got up and went on my way.

Chapter Thirty-Five

It's been a busy morning. I did the regular morning things and put the house back in order. After getting Rusty off to school, I did a load of laundry.

But my mind kept thinking about the computer and the possibilities. Wonder what would happen if I did a few sketches and took them to Mr. Whitman? Would he be interested in the kind of work I could do now? Or would it be better to send out some sketches to various fashion producers and see if I got a nibble?

Seems to me that the fashion scene is devoted too much to teens and young women. Middle aged women also want to look their best, and they may feel a little stupid trying to look like teenagers. And, of course, older ladies want to be attractive, but want their dignity, too. Someone should wake up to this market opportunity.

In the middle of my mulling these ideas, the phone rings.

"Hello."

"Yes, Angela?"

I could tell it was Mike so I said, "Present. What can I do for you?"

He chuckled and said, "Sounds like you are in a good mood. So how about meeting me for lunch? I don't have another appointment until two-thirty this afternoon, so I can have a little longer lunch break and would enjoy your company."

"Well -- that sounds interesting. Where do you want me to meet you? And when? It's a quarter to twelve right now."

"I know. I can't leave until twelve o'clock. But come as soon as you can. I may get there first. How do you feel about that quaint little restaurant on the Square – 'Dine with Pleasure'?"

"I've noticed it, but have never been there. It is very attractive. Just give me time to dress and I'll be there soon."

"What? You mean you aren't dressed at this time of day?" You could almost hear him grinning.

"Yes, Mr. Smarty. But I want to look my best if I'm going to such a fine place. Old slacks and a shirt might not make a good impression."

"Okay, but I'm already impressed. See you." And he hung up.

Mike has been our good friend for so long, but this seems a little unusual. Wonder what he has on his mind? Something connected with Rusty, I expect.

So I find a mid-length, cream-colored linen skirt with short, fitted jacket, and a pale pink sweater top. Then I apply a little make-up and give my hair some extra brushing. A little pink Barrett holds the top center section at the back of my head and the sides fall free. Not very fancy, but maybe I'll pass. There probably won't be many there at this time of day.

As I enter the restaurant, I see Mike at a far corner table toward the back of the room. He sees me and stands up.

As I approach, he pulls out my chair, like a real gentleman, and we sit. "I'm glad you could make it," he said, "and that we could have this table with the pretty view."

So I looked and he was so right. The lawn was immaculate, the trees in full leaf and all the flowers were blooming in perfectly designed plots. It was a scene that made one feel relaxed and comfortable.

When the waiter came, we both ordered iced tea, and began to check over the menu. Mike ordered the chicken-fried steak with all the extras, and I asked for a small salad and vegetable plate.

As we waited, we seemed to find it hard to come up with some little chit-chat, mostly looking out the window and making a few comments. I'm wondering what Rusty has told him, and if I'm in 'trouble'? I know they are very close, and I don't always know what Rusty is thinking, like I used to.

The food came and we were busy getting adjusted and getting started on the meal. Finally, I decided to make it as easy as possible for Mike. "What has my son been up to that worries you?" I asked.

Mike looked a little confused, then said, "Oh, no. I didn't ask you here to talk about Rusty. I'm sorry, I find it a little harder to get started than I thought it would be."

"Mike, we've been friends for many years and I doubt we have many secrets from each other. I don't think there is anything you could talk about that would surprise me."

But, boy, was I ever wrong!!

"Okay," he said. "I'll just barge right in. I believe you know how I feel about you. Don't see how you could help it since I hang around as much as possible. But if there is any doubt, I have to tell you that I have learned to love you and would like to have a much closer relationship with you. You know Rusty and I get along quite well. So that wouldn't be a problem. I'm hoping you feel the same about me, but if not, give me time and I'll convince you."

Actually, "surprised" is putting it very mildly. I was completely floored. I never expected anything like this.

"Ah -- Mike," I said. "I'm afraid this is a total surprise to me. I was very much in love with Chuck, as you were with your wife. That's one thing we have in common, the love we had for our companions. We are lonely people who have been good for each other. And you have been a special blessing to Rusty. No wonder he feels like you are his father. You are the most important man in his life. But I have been just drifting along, never considering marrying again. And to tell you the truth, I'm afraid I wouldn't be very good for you. Your religion seems to mean so very much to you. Yet, you know I don't feel the way you do. So, wouldn't that be a problem?"

"Yes, it could be. But you see, I have faith God can change your mind. I have been praying for that change for quite a long time. And I know some other people feel as I do, including Rusty. God is trying to touch your heart, but you keep running away."

Suddenly, I felt a cold chill and pulled my jacket closer. "Now, you are getting complicated," I said. "I don't think we'd better continue this discussion. I know who I am and how I feel. I thought you did, too. But as much as I care for you, Mike, you are asking too much of me. I know how God has treated me all these years and it's so plain to see that He cares nothing for me. I worked this out long ago, and have learned to live by depending only on myself. Please try to understand."

I fell silent. I know there were tears in my eyes. I didn't want to hurt Mike. He was such a wonderful person. It's just that he didn't understand.

Mike reached for my hand, and looked me straight in the eye. "I hear what you are saying, Angela. And it breaks my heart. But I have never been one to force myself on anyone and I won't start now. I hope we can continue as friends as we have been in the past, but I will never mention this to you again. If, by some miracle, you should change your mind or your heart, you can let me know. I'm not going anywhere. But I will not make a pest of myself."

I grabbed my Kleenex and stood up. "Thanks for lunch, Mike. Please don't drop Rusty. He needs you so much. We don't want to lose you."

"I'm not dropping anyone. I just needed to find out where I stood, and now that I know, I will act accordingly. You are welcome for lunch. I'll see you around."

I hurried away as quickly as I could.

~ ~ ~ ~ ~ ~ ~ ~ ~ ~ ~ ~

Things seemed to settle back into the normal day to day routine. But I couldn't help thinking about Mike and the scene in the restaurant. Over and over the words raced through my head. Yet I felt my answer had been the right one for all concerned.

Still, I felt guilty when Mike continued to come to dinner occasionally, or take us some place and continue to be a pal to Rusty. It seemed we were taking advantage of him somehow.

Chapter Thirty-Six

I need to get back to work. Now that I have begun to figure out a way to work with fashions, or it appears I have, I need to "get my feet wet," by venturing out.

So, bright and early, on Monday morning, after Rusty had gone to school, I sat at the computer and made a list of things that should be in my first presentation.

I wanted a handful of sketches that would catch the eye as being unique, yet with a dignity and charm. I decided this first attempt should be for the sixty to seventy-five age group. I jotted down some notes.

The first item was a sports outfit that included a pair of straight-legged pants with a flat, elastic waist band. There should be pockets and it would be made of a material, black or navy, weighted enough to hold its shape through repeated washings. The top would be the eye-catcher. It should be white with accents of black or navy to match the pants. The sleeves would be three-quarter length, ending with a deep, notched cuff that could be worn turned back and would be outlined in the matching color, black or navy. A line of black or navy buttons would march up the front of the blouse, which would be form-fitting and could be worn either in or out. The large, pointed collar, opened at the front leaving one or two buttons unbuttoned, would be outlined with black or navy and feature a small breast pocket which would show a design of the same color. This should make a simple, neat outfit for a relaxed life style.

My portfolio should also have an attractive dress for shopping or the office. Its skirt should be gored, fitting at the waist line, yet falling softly in a flare that moved as a person walked, and extended two inches below the knee. The top would be made from the same flowered, or printed silk-like material with a sheen and a drape that allowed it to fall softly from the slightly rounded neckline. An old-fashioned zippered placket at the waist line would allow the garment to be more form fitting. A matching belt and an optional scarf would complete this ensemble.

The final sample of the ladies' busy-life wardrobe would be an evening dress made of a silver sheen, soft draping material, that seemed to flow with movement. A floor length skirt and a modest, v-necked top with cap sleeves would complete the simple yet graceful dress. It could also be dressed up with jewelry if desired.

As I looked back over what I had written and visualized all of the things in my mind, I thought I had a good starting place. As I worked, no doubt, I would find ways to improve on the sketches. Now, to see what I could do.

~ ~ ~ ~ ~ ~ ~ ~ ~ ~ ~ ~

My first move was to find samples of the type of materials I felt matched the sketches best. So I made a quick trip to the wholesale house and began my search. I was not disappointed. My problem was that there was so much to choose from. Even materials used in garment manufacturing today are so much improved over what we used in the past.

After a search of about three hours, I finally decided on samples that I thought would be suitable, and rushed home to begin.

However, by now, the day was almost gone, so I decided to dream over the sketches that night, and stop now to prepare supper.

I thought Mike might come by, so I did a little extra. But he didn't show up. And I was surprised at how disappointed I felt. I mentioned to Rusty that I had expected Mike, but he was not concerned.

"No," he said. "I guess I forgot to tell you. He is meeting some of his friends he works with, and they are all going 'out' tonight. He seemed kind of excited about it. Hope he has a good time."

"Yeah, me, too." I said flatly. I should have known he could have a good time with other people. We aren't the only ones in his life. But it bothered me, and I couldn't figure out why.

~ ~ ~ ~ ~ ~ ~ ~ ~ ~ ~ ~

It was a couple of days before I got back to the sketches, what with one thing or another needing to be done. Then Becky stopped by one afternoon for a visit.

I decided to try out my ideas on her, and she encouraged me. Especially when she saw the samples of material, she got excited.

"Sure wish I could find something like that in the stores," she said. "I just get disgusted trying to find something that I'm not ashamed to wear in public. I have no doubt there will be a good market for your designs when you get started again."

That was music to my ears and inspired me greatly. I was eager to begin.

Making the sketches on the computer was a little more difficult than I had expected. I still had a lot to learn. I called Jim three times asking for advice. He is a kind fellow and seemed glad to help.

"I'm going to send you a bill for all this advice when you make your first million," he said. And I promised to pay promptly.

Finally, about three weeks later, I had some sketches that looked pretty good to me even with my poor eyesight. I attached swatches of suggested material to each sketch, slipped them into my briefcase and went to see Mr. Whitman.

Chapter Thirty-Seven

Mr. Whitman was in and I was able to see him almost as soon as I arrived. I have always admired him as a person, and have had great respect for his judgment and managing skills as I've watched him build Baker House into a profitable and prominent Fashion Corporation. His approval would give me a big boost.

"Angela, you are looking so well," he said, as he rose to greet me. "I see that old glow back in your cheeks and the spring in your step. You look great and I'm happy you are here. Does this mean you are ready to come back to work?"

This man doesn't waste time. That's one of his qualities that makes him so successful. But I have to disappoint him.

"Sorry, Mr. Whitman. I'm not able to come back to work. I do have some good news, though. The wonderful ophthalmologist who has been treating my eyes keeps up with all the new treatments and was able to get me into a trial for a new injection. And it was successful! Actually, it isn't available to the general public yet. But it has worked for me so far and I believe it will continue to be effective. It doesn't give back what I've lost in sight, but it stops the degeneration in its tracks. Although I have lost some ability to see, it shouldn't get any worse. So this puts me in a position to learn what I can do with what I have left. And I'm working on it."

"I'm learning to use a specialized computer program that helps me to sketch what's in my head. I still have a lot to learn, but I'm encouraged and hopeful that I may soon be able to do some worthwhile things." I paused for breath.

"So that explains the glow and the happy expression I see. I'm so glad. How can I help you?"

"Well, actually, I've brought you a set of sketches and suggestions and need your opinion. For one thing, could a seamstress operate from the computer sketches? I realize they are somewhat different from hand work."

"M - m - m," he mutters as he begins to look at the drawings. "Yes, I believe one could; maybe they need a little modification and an occasional written explanation. But I believe if you were working with a competent person, you should have no problems, or they would be minor and could be worked out."

"Thank you. That was the main thing that worried me. In hopes that it would be workable, I have made a small series of sketches, with suggested materials, and brought them for your evaluation. I'm very aware that the styles have changed drastically since I have been gone from the firm. But I am not pleased with what I see in the stores and have heard comments from other women that are also disappointed. When I walk down the street and see women, of all ages, so ridiculously dressed, trying to look like teenagers, my senses cry out in protest. Yet, I'm aware that they can buy only what is offered for sale. I believe a majority of mature women would dress better and more attractively, if something worthwhile were available. That's what I propose to do. Give them a choice they can live with."

Mr. Whitman listened intently.

"You've certainly given the matter a lot of thought and your arguments sound good. However, you may remember that the public doesn't always agree with what we think is what they need. So we try to give them what they want. And today, it seems, the theme is to 'look young,' even if you are eighty. So we have been going along with the trend for some time now. And it seems to work."

"I see no reason why looking young has to clash with looking respectable and attractive. I happen to think that women are more attractive dressing to fit their age and lifestyle. To me, it looks very disgusting to see a woman with gray hair and a bulging stomach wearing shorts and a halter. On the other had, if she were dressed appropriately for her age and size, she would appear as a lady of good taste and attractive appearance."

"Well, you have some good points in your argument. I assume you are proposing to design the things you think will cause the ladies to feel more comfortable and attractive than what is now available. Let me see what you have there."

I hand him my portfolio. "These were made with the sixty to seventy-five age group in mind," I said, then held my breath as he scanned through the proposals.

Finally, he looks up with a serious expression. "You have done some good work here, Angela. But, frankly, I doubt they would sell. Society is so relaxed these days. 'Comfort' is the next word after looking young. I'm sorry. Perhaps if you would do a little more research into today's market, you will be able to design attractive things that people will buy. But I believe they would consider these to be 'old fashioned.' As we are often reminded, this is the Twenty-First Century and everything must be different from the last century."

I was so disappointed, but I couldn't let him know. So I smiled as I gathered up my sketches and prepared to leave.

"Don't feel bad, Angela. And don't give up. You have accomplished a lot by learning to use the computer system. Keep doing your research and you will work it out in time."

I thanked him for his time and his opinion, and left as gracefully as I could.

Chapter Thirty-Eight

Mr. Whitman's evaluation of my work set me back on my heels for a time. It had been a shock, actually. I was prepared for his approval and suggestions of ways to get started with this new phase of my life. I had never thought he would say the things he did. But I had to give him credit. He had always been honest with me in the past. So I knew his opinions were what he believed the situation to be. The fact that I didn't see it that way, didn't change his beliefs. And, although, I was shaken by his words, deep inside I just knew I was right this time.

Because I respected Mr. Whitman, I decided to do just what he suggested. I planned to study the market more, make some surveys, check public opinion, review the fashion treads for the past and come up with conclusions that made sense at this time. It would take time and work, but it was all a part of the overall plan and would pay off in time.

My first stop was the library where I checked out several books to study at home. I had a friend in the Marketing Department of a large retail chain, and I arranged a meeting with her. I made a list of survey questions to put to my friends, and even strangers I might meet. Then I bought the latest fashion magazines. I would put all these things in the pot, stir them together, and see what I could come up with.

My mind was so involved with my "study program," that for days, I never once thought about Mike.

But when Sunday rolled around, I suddenly realized I hadn't heard from or seen him since our lunch meeting. Oh, well, he would come home with Rusty for Sunday dinner as usual. I would check on him then.

After Rusty left for church, I began to put together a "man-sized" meal of roast beef, vegetables, and salad, topped with lemon meringue pie. Then

I showered, dressed in a soft green street-length dress, with elbow-length sleeves and a sash. The pearls would just set it off. After an approving look in the mirror, I sat down with a magazine to await the arrival of 'my men'.

But when Rusty came in, Mike wasn't with him. "Where's the good doctor?" I asked.

"'Sir' dropped me off and is on his way to a tennis match this afternoon. When I said he should eat first, he told me he would pick up something at a café along the way. I don't know who he is playing with, but he seemed excited about it. I'm glad. For several days, he has seemed sort of 'down in the dumps.'"

Now I guess it was my turn to be "down in the dumps." Surprisingly, I missed him. What were we supposed to do with our Sunday afternoon? Rusty was off to do something with Willie and some other boys, but the long hours stretched before me.

I could read, or work on my project. But I was restless, and felt some vague sense of disappointment. What was the matter with me?

Chapter Thirty-Nine

Becky called to see if I was available for lunch. Said she had some things she wanted to run by me. I said, "Sure, I'll bring the soup, and you make us some of those great brownies. I'll be there at twelve, sharp."

This was just what I needed, a good talk with Becky. I had all that roast beef and vegetables left from yesterday's big dinner. I'd get everything simmering right away, and by lunch time, it would be delicious.

I poured two generous bowls of the soup, tucked them under my arm and headed for Becky's.

As I crossed the street, I wondered what she wanted to talk about. I certainly had a lot on my mind. So if she ran out of anything to say, I was prepared to jump right into the gap. That wasn't necessary. Becky had a whole afternoon's worth of things on her mind.

"What's up?" I asked.

"I have a couple of things I'd like to talk about," she said. She reminded me about their church project of collecting used clothing for underprivileged children. But there just didn't seem to be enough good things available. Some of the women had suggested that their Women's Group make some new things to give out as needed. Each woman would contribute the material and her work. Their problem was that they needed patterns for dresses, shirts, pants, and play clothes for children through fourth grade. She knew I would want to help.

She was right, of course. My mind jumped into high gear. Yes, yes, I thought. I could do that! I would make the designs and find a friend who could turn them into patterns. It would be great fun and I would be doing something worthwhile. The fact that I had not been doing anything for others was something that hadn't really bothered me in a long time. But suddenly, I wanted to be a part of this good project. I wanted to contribute. I thanked her for asking me. We would work out the details over the next few days and get started.

This, of course, would mean that I would have to interact with the church women. Would they accept me? Maybe... since I was Rusty's mother. They all seemed to have a soft spot for him.

This project worked out so well, I could hardly believe it. It was almost as if someone far wiser and more capable had planned the whole thing.

Because I was already familiar with designing on the computer, it didn't take long to come up with a number of good sketches. At the same time, I was learning more about design, and that wasn't bad.

When I took the designs to my friend, she, too, was excited about the project. By making all the different sized patterns for the various designs, we had quite a box full of patterns. I planned to pay for her work, myself. But she wouldn't hear of it. She wanted to contribute to such a good thing.

Of course, I couldn't sew. Didn't know how, and couldn't see well enough. But many were good seamstresses and they were eager to work. When they ran out of material, I could supply that. In fact, I still had my card and could buy wholesale. We were in business.

The project worked so well that in a few short weeks, we had an ample supply of neat and attractive clothing for both boys and girls.

All of us were proud of ourselves and planned to work together again when the need arose. At the same time, I met some great women and my circle of friends grew.

This was a winning situation for me, except for one thing. These were church women and they continually asked me to come to church. I didn't feel like I could explain my beliefs to them, so I would smile and thank them. But one day as they continued to talk about their thankfulness to God for making our project work, I wanted to scream at them --'No, No! God had nothing to do with it! We planned. We worked. God, if He exists, is not interested in our little project. Since He didn't hinder us, it may be that we slipped this in without His notice.' But of course, I couldn't say that out loud. They would never accept it.

As time passed and I had more contact with the church women, I began to hear little thoughts of a different kind. Being in the business of distributing clothing, they became aware of another need. The young children needed better schooling than they were getting. The poor parents had to work whenever they had an opportunity, and often that left children unattended. Many frequently missed school.

An idea was kicked around. Perhaps the church could sponsor a school for young children -- preschool through fourth grade.

Sounded good. But this involved a lot more than sewing two pieces of material together. It would cost a lot of money. They would need a building, or maybe even buildings. They would need accredited teachers, a school nurse, and a qualified administrator. Probably other needs that would arise in the course of time.

This was a fine little church, but they just didn't have that kind of money, or any means of getting it. I even gave it some thought myself, but I had no ideas of how to raise the money. Besides, it wasn't my problem. Let them ask their God. They believed He could do anything.

Chapter Forty

Willie stopped by. It was so good to see him. It had been a while. After finishing high school and college, he was now on his way to law school. Just stopped in to say a quick, "Good-bye."

He and I had been close all through his growing-up years, and I was almost as proud of him as if he were my own. As a child, he had befriended me at probably the lowest point in my life, and I loved him dearly. He had also been a great "big brother" to Rusty all these years, seeing after him, taking him to church, helping in so many ways.

Now he was almost ready to go out into the world to seek his fortune. Time had certainly slipped away. How could that cute, red-headed, freckled-faced little boy have turned into this handsome, confident young man while I was thinking about other things?

"Tell me about that cute, smart, beautiful girl friend of yours," I said.

"You mean, Janie?"

"I think so. How many cute, smart young women have you tricked into loving you?"

"Well, if you put it that way -- none. Janie is a great person, and we have had good times together. She's good for me in many ways. Helps me to keep my feet on the ground and not go off at a tangent. She's always cheerful and up-beat. But we aren't ready to settle down yet. She's gone back home to teach school. I'm hoping to get some more education and make a good name for myself as a lawyer. I'm thankful for Janie. We have made a good team. But we are going to be apart most of the time for the next few years, but anything can happen. We'll see."

"Oh, Willie, I admire your ambition and I have no doubt you will make a great name for yourself. But don't, my young friend, let love slip through your fingers. Love is probably the best thing that can ever happen to you. Once you find it, don't let it go."

"M, - m - m. Sounds like you know what you are talking about. It just doesn't match what I see."

"What do you mean? I've been in love and been loved. Chuck was a wonderful husband. I had no control over what happened and being left alone after his accident."

"Sure I know that. I'm not talking about ancient history. I'm thinking about how you are treating the good doctor. That man is in love with you. And I happen to believe you love him, too. But for some strange reason, you refuse to give him the time of day. You'll not find anyone better, I'll tell you that."

"Well, dear Willie 'Landers,' thanks for your advice. There's no doubt Dr. Mike is a wonderful person. But I'm not looking for a man. And if I were, I wouldn't want to mess up the life of a devout Christian who would have to accommodate himself to my beliefs, or rather non-beliefs."

"I'm sorry, Missy. It's really none of my business. I shouldn't have said anything. It's just that you are close to being the best friend I ever had, and I really do want you to be happy. But I have to say that I don't think you will ever be truly happy until you work through your problems with the Lord. But that's another subject." Then he continued, "I had better get on my way. I have several hours of driving ahead. I'll send you my address when I get settled. Maybe you can write once in awhile. I'll see you when I am able to come home. Good-bye, Missy."

He took my hand in both of his, then gave me a quick hug and he was gone.

I knew he and Rusty had said their "good-byes" last night. I sat for a long time, remembering Willie as a little boy, and what he had meant to me all these years. And I couldn't get his words about Mike out of my head. He was right, of course. But I just couldn't do it. Because I *do* love him, I couldn't put him through the sorrow of dealing with a wife who did not believe and was unable to participate in the things he valued most.

~ ~ ~ ~ ~ ~ ~ ~ ~ ~ ~ ~ ~

I still couldn't get Willie's words out of my mind, so Sunday morning, I told Rusty to ask Mike to come to dinner. I was not yet ready to greet him with open arms, but he was a good friend to both of us and I had missed him lately.

I was pleased to see both Rusty and Mike step from the car and turn toward the house, after the morning services.

Mike seemed at ease, and was cordial. But there was no peck on the cheek as I used to get. Dinner was good, if I do say so, and both of them ate as if they were enjoying every bite. Of course, that always cheers a cook's heart and I felt we were making progress in getting things back together.

"How was bowling last night?" Rusty asked Mike.

Mike sat a little straighter and smiled. "Great," he said. "My team really 'smashed' them! Now they want a rematch. We'll probably let them 'have it' again next Saturday night."

This was the first I'd heard about bowling. "Who's on your team?" I asked.

" Oh, the people I work with. Some of the doctors, nurses, and other personnel. Whoever happens not to have anything better to do. The same people are not always on the same team. We draw numbers each week. You are on Team One or Two -- whichever number you draw. Works out better that way, and keeps it more of a fun thing than a battle. Good exercise. I'm glad Nurse Sandy asked me to join. She's been good at helping me perfect my swing, too. But that's enough about my social life."

Dr. Mike changed the subject. "How are things going with you, Angela? Sold any sketches yet? I know you are good. Just keep working on it. You'll make a fortune some day." He paused for breath.

"As a matter of fact," I said, "I have no desire to make a fortune. But I do expect to make a difference in the fashion scene one day. I believe in my ideas and I believe in the good sense of the women I'm hoping to serve. I'm very confident."

"That's good," he said. Then, turning to Rusty, he asked about his soccer team's standing in their High School League. And they were off on sports, and both seemed to completely forget that I was there.

So after dinner, they went off to check on something they had been discussing and I was left with the dirty dishes and a book. Not much for all the work I had put into the meal.

Chapter Forty-One

As I took stock of my current situation, I considered several things.

My son, around whom my life had existed for the last seventeen years, would soon be launching out on his own. He would be more independent, therefore I must be, too. I wasn't that old and still had a life to live.

If Chuck were here, this would be our good time together. We would be involved in our work, yet have time to "see the world," so to speak. But long ago, I had accepted the fact that our life together was over. Yes, it was finished, and I had done well in rebuilding my life up to this point. How happy I was that my eyesight, while still a problem, had turned out not to be complete blindness and I still had the ability to see to a workable degree. So work would be my answer from now on.

While I valued Mr. Whitman's judgment, I believed in myself more. I knew there was a market for the type of things I would design. All I had to do was make them available and the buyers would come.

Of course, it would take time, planning, and lots of work. But that was what I enjoyed. I had the talent, the ability, and the means to make it happen. I would use some of the money Chuck had left me. The amount I needed would scarcely be missed, but it would enable me to make my dream come true.

First, I needed to call Mr. Brown and make an appointment to withdraw the money I would need. He would see me Wednesday morning at ten-thirty.

I also needed a building in a suitable location. Of course, I could do the designs at home, but it would be better if we could keep the whole operation under one roof. Where would I find a good real estate agent?

The yellow pages? Maybe. I will ask Becky and her church ladies. Perhaps they had connections.

I hoped the old friends I had made at the wholesale houses, and perhaps some of the equipment companies when I worked for Baker House, might still be around. There was certainly a lot involved in starting a business.

After talking with Attorney Brown and getting his blessing, I was encouraged. But when I got an estimate of the funds I would need just to start, I almost gave up. All I wanted to do was design attractive clothes, and I was already bogged down in a lot of details.

Becky stopped by and it was a relief to have a few minutes just to "chit-chat" with my old friend. During our talk, she mentioned her daughter, Jean. I knew Jean had studied accounting and was now working on her own. Becky told me she was doing quite well, with three people working for her. They did general audits for a number of businesses, and also maintained the day to day bookkeeping for several small firms. I was impressed. This attractive young lady had a good head on her shoulders and might just be the one to help me get organized in my business venture.

I asked her Mother for her phone number and contacted her that afternoon. Jean became excited the minute I mentioned the new business and told me she would really like to set up an accounting system for our venture. She insisted that getting it right, at the beginning, was the key to having a good system that would allow one to keep informed about whether or not this was a profitable venture.

~ ~ ~ ~ ~ ~ ~ ~ ~ ~ ~ ~ ~

Jean Rogers went with me to the bank to open the account in which Mr. Brown was to place the first $100,000. We had agreed to start small, with the assurance that more money was available when needed.

The real estate agent had located a suitable building very near the residential part of the city, yet near enough to downtown to make it a part of the shopping scene.

The upper floors were adequate for the production space, for designing, pattern making, cutting, sewing, etc.

The main floor would be the show room where we would display and sell our productions.

Sounded simple. Actually, it took many weeks of work on my part, and I had pled with Becky until she had agreed to help.

There was work space to set up. Equipment to buy. Workers to hire.

Finding the seamstresses was quite the easiest of all. Several of the church ladies who had worked on the children's clothing project were eager to have a paying job, doing something they enjoyed.

My old friend, the pattern maker, recommended two of her young assistants. I set up an account with the Fabric House, and we were practically ready to begin the venture.

During this time, I had been making some sketches of various types of clothing that we planned to manufacture.

Finally our business was underway. I handed the sketches to the pattern makers, who passed the patterns on to the cutters, and the material was soon on its way to the seamstresses. The first day a garment was completely finished, pressed, and hung for approval, we all celebrated and took the rest of the day off.

Soon the operation took off. Our storeroom was filling with completed garments, and it was time to open our exclusive shop on the main floor. Two experienced clerks had been lured away from their positions downtown so our retail shop was now open for business, too!

Chapter Forty-Two

Actually we were doing better in business than I had dreamed. I would have liked to tell Mr. Whitman, but I didn't want to gloat. This was the only time I'd known him to make a misjudgment, and it probably would never happen again. In fact, if I hadn't known better, I would have thought God was blessing our efforts. Since I knew that couldn't be, I took a little credit for myself.

But I didn't down play the work of others, from Becky and her supervisory skills, to the girl who kept our floors clean and the displays in neat order. It was a combined effort. And all of us were happy. As profits increased, so did salaries. I didn't take out much for myself. I didn't need it. Also, I wanted to encourage the workers.

I had been so busy getting things going that I had all but neglected my son and friends.

One day I woke up to the fact that I hadn't seen Mike in three weeks, and I wondered about him. When I asked Rusty, he didn't say much. The doctor had been busy. He seemed to have a new circle of friends and Rusty apparently was feeling left out. I couldn't imagine that. They had been so close, so long.

I decided it was time I checked things out. So I called Mike and asked him to come to supper one night. He started to give me an excuse, then seemed to think better of it. "Okay," he said. "I'll be there at six."

That left me with a funny, empty feeling, but I got right to work to prepare a meal he could never turn down.

Rusty seemed surprised when I told him Mike was coming. But he was glad, also. "Great," he said. "I have several things I need to talk to him about."

After supper, we sat around the table a little while, catching up on this and that. Mike looked so good. He had developed a tan. Tennis? Maybe. He seemed at ease, although I caught him casting a sideways glance at me now and then.

Finally he and Rusty wandered away from the table into the living room, where I heard them settle into easy chairs. I cleared the table and put the dishes in the dishwasher to do later.

I heard the last of their conversation as I approached. Mike was saying, " -- I'm so very proud of you. I know you will stick with it, but you are right, making a public commitment is always good."

Mike got up when I entered, but I motioned him back down. I sat on the edge of the couch. All was quiet for a minute, then Mike turned to me.

"Well, Angela, how's the big business going? I must tell you I've heard some mighty favorable comments from some of my patients."

"Thanks, Mike. I think we're getting geared up to really make a difference. And there is a lot of satisfaction in that. Also, the people involved seem happy and work well together. Oh, I know, we're just getting started. But it's a good start, and with any luck, we should be a great success one day."

Mike gave me a strange look, then said, "Well, that's good."

I knew he was uncomfortable for some reason, so I asked, " What have you been up to lately? We've missed you around here."

"Oh, the usual, I guess. A lot of work. But I've been thinking I should try to make something of myself instead of just being a workaholic and 'a drag on society.' I've been getting out more. Meeting new people. Sandy, one of our nurses, has been teaching me tennis. And it is really good for me. Good for the old body, but also for the mind and spirit. Even makes me feel younger, something I haven't felt in a long time."

As he paused for breath, I said, "Well, I'm happy for you Mike. You deserve some real happiness. But we've missed you. Guess we grew to depend on you too much. Probably should take a page out of your book and start making some changes in my personal life. Although I really don't seem too have a personal life any more" -- I slowly wound down and looked away. Suddenly I felt very cold, -- and alone.

Mike began to rise with his hand outstretched, then just as suddenly, withdrew his hand and sat back down.

We looked at each other for a minute, then I turned away. I sure didn't want him to see the tear in my eye.

Mike stayed a little longer, and we chatted back and forth for a while, but he soon left, pleading he had to get an early start in the morning.

As we said our "good-byes," I felt completely drained. Didn't even have the heart to go turn on the dishwasher.

Rusty seemed totally unaware of my discomfort and turned to me expectantly. "Mom," he said. "I've been doing a lot of thinking lately, and after talking with 'Sir,' I believe I know what I should do. In two weeks, we will have 'Dedication Sunday' at church. We do this about once a year. It's a time for lost people to be saved, for those who have wandered away to come back, and for others to make a special dedication of their lives. This year, I'm going to dedicate my life to full-time service for the Lord."

Startled, I looked up. "What do you mean? I always thought you were going to be an architect, but never a preacher."

"Sure, Mom, I've always known I am to be an architect, but I will be a better architect if I'm in full-time service for the Lord. Anything I design will be for His glory as well as being useful or beautiful. Don't you see? It will be my ministry to, and for Him."

I needed time to think abut this, but I didn't want to discourage him. "Well, if that is what you want to do," I said, "it sounds all right to me."

"Thanks, Mom. And as a special favor, will you come that day to stand by me in my decision. Life can be hard sometimes. I will still need you. And I want to call Grandpa. I think he would like to be here. What do you think?"

Although in a daze, I assured him that would be fine. And soon he went happily off to bed, dreaming big dreams, no doubt.

I sat for a long time, puzzling the events of the evening. Finally, I got up, started the dish washer and went off to an uneasy sleep.

Chapter Forty-Three

The next morning, I got up early and went off to the shop where I could find peace, for a while, in my work. I was working on a new Spring outfit that could be copied in different fabrics and colors to appeal to different color types and positions in life. It was interesting to see the different variations that could be made from the basic pattern.

As I worked, my mind drifted back over the years. I remembered my early days in the City and my elation at landing the job at Baker House. I was so young. I thought I had the world in my hand and would form it to suit myself.

When I married Chuck, with my work soaring off into the heights, I knew I was already successful. Only a wonderful life lay ahead. How ignorant I was!

With Chuck's untimely death, everything changed. I never understood about grief until them. When I began losing my sight and expecting a baby, I panicked. Dad tried to help but his answer to everything was to trust God, the same God who had forsaken me years before.

The years have been hard in many ways. Loneliness had played a large part. Of course I had Rusty, and Becky helped so much. Then there was Mike. Oh, Mike! I really do love him, of course. And now I have probably lost him, too. But how could I saddle him with a wife who did not share his religious beliefs?

There was nowhere to turn except back to myself, as always. Rusty would be leaving soon and I would be right back where I started more than twenty years ago.

This new business was my salvation, of course. I would put all my energies into it and it would repay me with success.

One of the girls came by my desk and asked what I was doing. As I explained some of the sketches, I could sense her approval.

"This is great!" she said. "I can hardly wait to get started on them."

And I felt a sense of satisfaction. And confidence. I still had "it." I could manage my life as I always had.

Let them all leave me. Forget about their God. Angela Graham could take care of herself.

Suddenly, I felt a chill, although it was warm in the building. I sat and stared into space, frightened and alone.

~ ~ ~ ~ ~ ~ ~ ~ ~ ~ ~ ~ ~

When I arrived home, all was quiet. I found Rusty's note telling me he wouldn't be home for supper, but wouldn't be real late. He and a buddy were working on some material at the library.

I should visit the library, myself. I always found some good ideas there. Well, maybe tomorrow. Now I needed to do something about this headache. I don't know where it came from. I was doing fine a few hours ago, when suddenly it hit and I felt alone and confused. A good night's sleep would take care of it, although I might have to take something.

The ringing of the telephone startled me. I was pleased when I heard Mike's voice.

"Hi, Angela. Hope I didn't disturb you."

"Of course not. I just got home a little while ago and found a note from Rusty saying he wouldn't be home until later. So I was just looking about for something to eat that doesn't take much effort to prepare."

"Good. I caught you at the right time. How about I pick you up and we go to the corner diner for hamburgers? I haven't had a good hamburger in a long time."

"Sounds wonderful," I said. Then I realized my headache was gone.

"This is a 'come-as-you-are' party," Mike said. "I'll be at your house in about ten minutes."

Ten minutes gave me time to freshen up a bit and then I waited on the front porch.

Mike was in great humor as we talked and laughed and enjoyed our hamburgers. Afterwards, he suggested that we drive around a bit, and I agreed. It was a pleasant evening. Just what I needed.

We didn't go any place special. Just drove around town in the residential section and out past the lake. I felt so good, so peaceful.

Finally, Mike spoke. "Rusty tells me you are coming to the Dedication Service on Sunday when he makes public his decision for full-time Christian service."

I had almost forgotten that. Of course Dad would have reminded me when he arrived in a couple of days. It wasn't something I really wanted to do, but felt I had to support Rusty.

"Well, yes." I said. "It seemed so important to him. I guess I don't understand exactly what he means by 'full-time,' but he seemed confident and happy about the situation. I'm wondering if he thinks this is going to assure him of God's help in his work? I sure would hate to see him get disappointed as I have been."

"Oh, Angela!" Mike gave me a funny look. Then he was quiet for a while. I realized I had probably said the wrong thing, but it was the way I felt.

But in a few minutes we were back on good terms and nothing more was said about the Sunday Service.

When Mike took me home about nine o'clock, I felt so good, so relaxed. This outing with him had been just what I needed.

I turned to Mike with a smile on my face and began, "Dear Mike! I've missed you so. This evening was great. I have spent most of the day looking back and trying to figure out where I go from here, with Rusty moving on and things changing. You have given me comfort and new courage. I know, now, I'll manage somehow."

When I looked at his face, I quickly realized I'd said the wrong thing again.

"Yes, I'm sure you will manage," he said dully. " See you Sunday at the service. Goodnight." He drove quickly away.

~ ~ ~ ~ ~ ~ ~ ~ ~ ~ ~ ~ ~

Dad arrived a couple of days later, and we've had a great time visiting together. It's been a while since he was last here, and I can see some differences in his movements. He is slower now. And not so eager to dash outside and do a little work on the yard. These last twenty years have brought about many changes in all of us.

Rusty has grown up into a fine young man, with a good head on his shoulders, and great plans in his mind.

My friendship with Becky, her husband, and her children, has ripened into the closest of relationships, like family. I've become acquainted with many good people who have added to my life. I've realized my dream of my own fashion company. And the eyesight I believed gone forever, even though limited somewhat, is still here helping me do the many things I enjoy.

I have not forgotten Chuck and the brief, great time we had together. There's Rusty to remind me, of course. And there's also Mike. Dear Mike. How I wish I could be what he wants me to be.

But the years have taught me over and over that I can, and must, depend on myself. I certainly cannot rely on some distant God who, long ago, made it plain He cared nothing for me.

Mike just can't understand that. So I guess if it works for him, so be it.

Chapter Forty-Four

The Sunday for he Dedication Service dawned bright and clear. A beautiful day.

I'd had my hair done the day before. A special treat. I would wear my new spring outfit that I designed myself. It was a form-fitting dress of blue-flowered silk print with a sleeveless three-quarter, flowing navy linen coat, decorated with embroiled blue and white flowers on both sides of the open front. I wanted Rusty to be proud of me.

Mike was a bit early when he came to pick up our little group for the service. But we certainly wanted to be on time.

Rusty sat up front with Mike, and Dad and I climbed into the back seat of Mike's shinny, late model car. And we were off.

It wasn't far. As I climbed out of the car, I looked about and remembered the few times I had been here before, over the years. The building seemed larger now, and very neatly appointed. May have been enlarged to accommodate the growing crowds, and the new designs and decorations were very attractive.

We seated ourselves in the auditorium, not far from the front. Rusty planned to be available when the time came.

Soon the auditorium began filling with many other folks. The choir appeared. The orchestra quietly tuned their instruments.

There was a hush as the pastor mounted the platform, and a feeling of anticipation in the air. This was new to me and made me a little uncomfortable.

Following the opening prayer by the pastor, the congregation sang two old hymns. The ushers came forward to take the offering.

Quiet followed as a young girl arose to sing a special. I would guess she was about seventeen, very simply dressed in a pink sheath, with a white corsage at her shoulder. Her long, blond hair appeared to have a natural wave as it draped softly about her face. Her clear, lilting voice reached out to us as she sang with conviction, "I have decided to follow Jesus. No turning back. No turning back." Then she slipped easily into "Make me a channel of blessing, I pray. My life possessing, my service blessing. Make me a channel of blessing today." She bowed her head quietly for a minute as the organ music faded away. The room was still.

The pastor stepped behind the pulpit, as his gaze swept the congregation gathered there. The room appeared to be full. He began, "Today has been set aside as Dedication Sunday. At the close of our service, you will be given an opportunity to respond. It is a time for those who realize they are lost, undone, with no hope of eternity, to put their trust in the Lord for salvation."

"The Holy Spirit has been working with some of you for a while and perhaps this is the day you will say, 'Yes' to God and become His child for all eternity. There are others here today who have accepted Christ as their Savior, but have failed to do the first thing He asked each of us to do. You may want to join the church, asking for baptism, and get to work for the Lord."

The pastor continued, "Then there are probably some here who once enjoyed a close relationship with God, but for various reasons, have wandered away and no longer try to follow His will and way in their lives. If you are one of those, today is the accepted time. Now you can return to God and seek His guidance and care again. He is waiting for you."

"Also, this is a time for those who feel they want to dedicate their lives to special service for the Lord, to make it known. There is something for each of us here today. May the Holy Spirit guide you as you listen and make your decision."

"Let us now turn to the fifteenth chapter of Luke's Gospel and begin reading with the eleventh verse:

> *A certain man had two sons. And the younger of them said to his father, "Father, give me the portion of goods that falleth to me. And he divided unto them his living."*

Right away, I recognized the story of the prodigal son. I had heard it many times before. We studied it in Sunday School, and the pastor preached on it sometimes. Old stuff. I knew the story. So my mind slipped into neutral as he read on. Suddenly I heard,

> *"And when he came to himself, he said.....I will arise*

and go to my Father....But when he was yet a long way off, his father saw him, and had compassion on him, and ran and fell on his neck and kissed him......But the father said to his servants, "Bring forth the best robe and put it on him, and put a ring on his hand, and shoes on his feet."

Something jabbed me in my chest, and I realized tears were streaming down my face. Was I the prodigal? Had I gone to a far country and wasted my talent and my years that I could have lived for the Lord?

I was so sure I had been right! I never thought God loved me, and had grieved because I had turned my back on Him. But He had been waiting, and now, he was reaching out to me. He was welcoming me home.

Oh, how guilty I felt. 'I am no more worthy to be called your child,' I cried silently. 'I have spoken against you, ignored you, and refused to follow you, all these years. But you are welcoming me back. Oh, God, I never knew such love as that. Yes, I want to come home. I want to be the person you planned me to be. Help me, Father, to find my way.'

All of these things I was thinking and was unaware that I was walking slowly toward the front of the room.

By this time, the pastor had finished his remarks and was praying that the people would respond to God's invitation to do His will in their lives.

When I managed to look up, I saw that a number of other people were standing with me. Many of them were weeping. All were quiet and solemn.

The pastor began talking with the people to his left, the other end (from me) of the semicircle of folks standing in front. Each person was asked to make a statement about why they were there.

Of course this was hard for everyone, some more than others. I couldn't prepare myself for what I should say.

The first was a little boy, about ten years old. He sobbed, "I want Jesus to be my Savior." The pastor shook his hand, patted him on the back and assured him that Jesus loved him and was now his Savior forever. Along the way, others echoed the little boy's words in one way or another. A number of people came for church membership, some moving their letters and others for baptism.

Suddenly, it was my turn. I stood there with tears streaming down my face, unable to speak for a minute. Then I could feel the words in my mouth and knew God would help me say what I needed to say.

"I am the Prodigal Son, or Daughter," I said. "For many years I have been in a far country, and didn't really realize where I was. When I was a child, God saved me. But when my Mother died, I turned my back on God, claiming He no longer cared for me and I refused to acknowledge Him, if He even existed. As I look back over the years now, it's easy to see how He continued to love me, care for me, and patiently wait for my return. I am so sorry, so ashamed, and so happy that He has welcomed me home again."

As I stopped speaking, I realized the room was quiet. Then a long sigh filled the air, and I heard a number of "Amen's" and others say, "Thank you, Lord."

Mike put his arm around me on one side and Rusty on the other. And Dad was on his knees at my feet, thanking God for my return.

Finally the pastor spoke to the congregation, "This is something for which many of us have prayed for a long time. This young lady won our hearts many years ago, but she was blind to God's love and it seemed we would never be able to reach her. This is a Day of Thanksgiving."

"But we have one more person to hear from, a young man who grew up in our midst, trusting the Lord at an early age, growing in grace and knowledge most of his life. Rusty Graham has something to tell us."

As the room grew quiet again, Rusty looked over the congregation and smiled. "Everybody who is happy, say, Amen." he said enthusiastically. A loud, "Amen!" followed.

"Thank you. I knew you loved my Mother and we are all thankful for her realization that God loves her, too."

"Now, about me. I guess everyone knows I want to be an architect. I've worked in that direction all my life and am now am about to go away to school to learn more about how to be the best I can be. But I am here today to dedicate myself and my work to God's glory. I pray He will guide me and help me to be a blessing to others. At the same time, I want everyone to know I'm not working for fame and fortune, but for my Heavenly Father. I want the things I do to bring honor to Him. So I am dedicating my life to special service. That old hymn, 'Where Ever He leads, I'll Go,' will be my motto."

There was a lot of applause and a number of those in the congregation saying, "Amen." "We'll, pray for you, Son." "Praise God."

Suddenly, quiet filled the building as the pastor approached the pulpit.

"What a wonderful day the Lord has given us," he said. "I know you are all emotionally excited, but tired. We will have our closing prayer, and then I ask you to come forward and shake the hands of these good folks who have made life-changing decisions today. Wish them God-Speed and dedicate yourselves to pray for them. God is so good!"

He bowed is head. His prayer was brief.

The people came forward, clasping our hands and giving us hugs. Many happy tears flowed.

As the crowd began to thin out, the four of us walked slowly to Mike's car. We all seemed to be reluctant to leave this holy place.

Dad suggested we stop at the cafeteria on the way home. "We're late today," he said. "The Methodists will be finished by now." We all laughed.

Chapter Forty-Five

In the days that followed, a number of changes took place in our lives.

Mike wasted no time in getting my promise to marry him soon. Dad needed to go home, but promised to be back in time for the wedding. And Rusty was making his final preparations to go off to college.

It was a busy household, with little time to spare for daydreaming. But early one morning, Rusty asked me to go with him to look at something.

I couldn't imagine what he was thinking as we went back to the church. We parked and walked around the building. Behind the church was a large area of level ground, perhaps two or three acres. Large oak trees were scattered here and there. Also, there were a few bushes, and a wide, grassy area.

"What do you think, Mom?" he asked. "Wouldn't this be a good place for the Preschool and Beginners school building that we've all talked about?"

"Yes, it seems ideal," I said. "But the land doesn't belong to the church, does it?"

"Not yet, but I was hoping you might want to buy it so the church could use this tract to build a school."

"M - m - m. Let me think about it. Who owns it?"

"Mr. Wilson, the man who lives in that big house on the corner. I've talked to him and he would be willing to sell the acreage to the church for a school."

"Been a busy little fellow, haven't you? Do you know how much he wants for it?"

"No, but he said he would be reasonable. I think he has a soft spot for the church."

"Give me a few days to see what I can do. There aren't any other buyers lined up, are there?"

"Not that I know of. But if I went off to school, knowing the land was waiting, I could start making architectural plans and perhaps get a little help from some other people who know more than I do about this type of facility."

"Okay," I said. "There are a few people I need to talk to. But we'll see what can be done."

I had a plan, but I needed to get the approval of my workers at the shop.

Some time ago, the ladies who worked at the shop, with Becky as the spokesperson, had come to me with the suggestion that they put the tithe from their salaries back into the business, and watch it grow. When a need came up, they could cash in and have a good sum of money to do something worthwhile. Maybe the time had come.

~ ~ ~ ~ ~ ~ ~ ~ ~ ~ ~ ~ ~

I passed Becky's work station and asked if she had time for lunch.

She was delighted. "Of course. I'm always ready to eat."

We went to a little restaurant down the street and found a booth in the back corner. After placing our orders, Becky turned to me.

"What's up?" she asked. "Are we in trouble?"

"Not that I know of. What have you been up to that you haven't told me?"

She gave me a serious blank look. "I can't think of a thing."

I laughed. "Just kidding," I said. "It's not what you have done that I want to talk about. It's something you may want to do."

Then I explained about the property for the school and that I considered it a worthy project for the ladies, if they should agree. I was willing to go to Mr. Wilson, who owned the property, and help work out the deal if they wanted me to.

"But I thought it best, Becky if you presented the idea to the ladies. You know them much better than I do and I don't want to pressure them into doing something they don't really want to do, or don't think is the wise thing to do. I realize there are a lot more hurdles to jump before the school we have in mind could be built. But getting the land is the first step. If you and the other ladies bought the land, then you could give it to the church with the provision that it be used for the school and campus. I would suggest that as a step to protect your donation."

"Wow," Becky exclaimed. Then she sat very still for a minute with a far away look in her eye. "That's been a dream of mine for many years. It wouldn't benefit my children, but I believe it would be a blessing to the younger children of our community. You know my feelings abut some of the things that are happening in the public schools. Let me go home and talk to Eddie. We'll pray about it, and if it continues to seem as good as it sounds to me right now, I'll talk to the girls after work tomorrow. Would you get Jean to give us an estimate of how much money we have?"

"Sure," I said. But I already had a pretty good idea, and I knew it was ample.

So I would await the results of the meeting and then be off to see Mr. Wilson if the ladies agreed. I was eager to complete this deal before Rusty left home.

~ ~ ~ ~ ~ ~ ~ ~ ~ ~ ~ ~ ~

As I expected, the women in the shop were willing to withdraw their funds and purchase the property. And true to his word, Mr. Wilson was willing to accept a much smaller sum than he would have charged anyone else. It was a beautiful piece of property and would make a lovely campus.

Yes, I know, I could have used some of the money Chuck left for me, but this way, it would mean much more to the staff of the shop as they worked together. My money would be needed when we begin to build. By the time we were ready, my inheritance should be sufficient to build and equip an adequate building.

But I knew this was only the beginning. We would need an administrator, teachers, nurse, lunch room workers, janitors, etc. And salaries would be a continuing thing. I wondered if the church could put the upkeep of the school into its regular budget. A lot of things to think about. But Rusty was happy, knowing the land was secure. He had big dreams.

This project was also exciting to everyone else and a lot of day-dreaming went on. One day, I had to remind the ladies we were in the business of designing and manufacturing clothing and we still needed to make a profit. They laughed, and got back to work quickly. They knew what they were here at the shop for, and the school property gave them renewed incentive to make good.

~ ~ ~ ~ ~ ~ ~ ~ ~ ~ ~ ~ ~

A surprise call from Mr. Whitman one morning shook me up. I couldn't imagine why he would call.

"Angela, my dear, how are things going?"

"Quite well, I think, Mr. Whitman. How about with you?"

"Oh, fine, fine. Say, would you have time to talk with me if I came over to your office this morning?"

"Of course," I replied. "Come any time." I was more puzzled than ever.

Soon the secretary showed Mr. Whitman into my office and I did what I could to make him comfortable.

He looked around carefully. "A very nice place you have here, Angela. Do you suppose I could take a tour of the work area?"

"Sure. I'll show you around, myself. We are proud of our operation and our contribution to the fashion world."

"Yes, of course. You sure proved me wrong, didn't you? I just didn't think the public would accept your ideas of more graceful and attractive clothing. Everyone seemed so set on being sportive, laid back, and relaxed. But you were right. Many were searching for more attractive apparel and you filled that need."

"Thanks for your kind words. I wasn't trying to prove you wrong. You are one of the best friends I've ever had in the business world. In fact, most of what I know, I learned from you. It's just that I had talked with a number of women who were searching for something better, and I felt the market was out there. Fortunately, that was true."

After taking a tour of the work space and the show room, we went back to my office. I offered Mr. Whitman a cup of coffee, which he seemed grateful to accept. We sat quietly for a couple of minutes, while he sipped the coffee and looked out the window.

Then he turned and looked at me for a moment. "Angela," he said, "How would you like to come back home?"

I guess I looked startled. I couldn't think of what he meant. "I don't understand," I said. "This shop is 'home' now, for work. We have a great organization and each woman is good at what she does. Also each one has a financial interest in our making good."

"Sure, it was my idea at first, and I had the financial resources to get started. But these people are my friends and each one has a share in the work. They have each invested part of their salary into the business and have been able to do something worthwhile with the profits. I couldn't just desert them. Besides me, we have two other designers who are doing excellent work. So I don't do much of that now, but I do think they look to me to hold things together."

"M - m - m, I see." he said. He sat quietly for a few minutes, staring out the window.

"You have an excellent operation here and I believe I understand how it works.

What I'd really like to do is make this organization a branch of Baker House. You would run the operation here as you do now, but we would put our label on the finished merchandise, and sell it through our already established markets. We would have no trouble selling everything you could produce. Probably there would be additional profits since we are an old established firm."

"In exchange for that, we would keep everyone in place, raise salaries and allow the women to continue to invest as they have in the past. They would be free to decide at what point they wanted to make their withdrawals and the money would be used."

This was so unexpected that I suppose I sat there with my mouth open for a few minutes.

"Mr. Whitman, this is such a surprising offer, that I'm at a complete loss. Nothing like this has ever crossed my mind. Of course, I will have to talk with the ladies and explain your offer. I have no idea how they will feel about it. I know they are very proud of their work and what they have been able to accomplish. But I owe it to them, and to you, to present the offer. I'll let you know their answer in a few days."

Mr. Whitman left soon, with a smile on his face, and said that he hoped we would be able to work out something that would be good for both parties.

Chapter Forty-Six

Becky was waiting for me one morning about a week later when I got to the office.

"Good morning, Early Bird." I said.

"And a good morning to you, Boss."

"Okay, kid. Let's have it. What's the verdict? Are the ladies willing to accept Mr. Whitman's offer?"

"Well," she paused. "Maybe." Another pause. I waited.

"It's like this," she said. "We all think it would give our work a boost to carry the Baker House label and probably sales would go up, and so would our salaries. So that part sounds good. We just don't think the offer is good enough."

"All of us are still thinking about the Church School, and even though you have told us you already have the money lined up for the building and equipment, we know that the upkeep, including salaries, will be an ongoing thing. What we could set aside would help some, but it would not be nearly enough. My dear Eddie suggested that we need some kind of endowment that would assure yearly income."

They had all been doing some serious thinking here, and I was very pleased. I had realized we needed more backing but I hadn't come up with any ideas.

"So, continued Becky, "the thing is -- it looks to us like Baker House is going to get an 'up and running' subsidiary for practically nothing. While the profits would be more, Mr. Whitman's firm would realize them from our work. What we propose is that Baker House set up a Foundation to accumulate the needed endowment funds for the School, as part of our deal. We believe Baker House could afford to donate a large chunk of the funds themselves, but they also have influence with a number of other businesses who could contribute. I don't know all the legal stuff that would have to be involved, but I'm sure they have people in place to handle that. So what do you think?" She took a deep breath and sat back in her chair.

"What do I think? I think you have come up with an outstanding idea that should be fair, and profitable, to all concerned. I'm glad you have Eddie for guidance, but I now know where he gets his wisdom. There's no doubt God is guiding us here. I'll call Mr. Whitman right away and see if I can get the ball rolling. I have no reason to believe he will not agree. It's still a small price to pay for what the Baker house would be getting."

"The other employees and I realize you were the one who put up the money in the first place to start this operation. We could have never done any of it without you and you will never get much of a return on your money."

"Oh, quite the contrary. I am the one who benefits most. My son is so excited that his first architectural project will be to design a school building. He certainly has a lot to learn, but he is headed to college in just a few days. He also believes he can get some expert help because it is a 'real' and worthwhile project. Also, I have the satisfaction of having a part, like the rest of you, in helping to get the job done. As we all now know, money isn't the most important thing in the world. But we will talk Mr. Whitman out of as much of it as we can." I laughed, but I was very serious.

When I called and asked if we could talk about the merger, Mr. Whitman suggested that we talk over lunch.

~ ~ ~ ~ ~ ~ ~ ~ ~ ~ ~

We met at the Oak Lawn Restaurant, one of the swanker places in town. The meal was delicious and we enjoyed visiting and remembering old times. Mr. Whitman was extremely pleased that the experiment on my eye had been successful and that I hadn't lost all my sight completely. I tried to tell him it was part of God's plan for my life, but he apparently didn't understand, and didn't pursue it as he had been familiar with my attitude in the past.

After the waiter had removed the dishes, Mr. Whitman leaned back in his chair. "Okay, young lady. Let's have it. I have a feeling there is a catch in your counter proposal somewhere."

"Well, it isn't a 'catch', exactly," I said. "It's just that after thinking it over, the women think they would be in just abut the same position as they are now, but that you would have a ready-made new operation set up to make more profit for Baker House."

"It's not that they object to your making a profit from their work. They realize that's what it's all about. But there is something they want in return."

"I'll admit it is a little unusual and you may not want to agree to it, or your Board may have some objections, but to me, it seems reasonable and fair.

"Our workers are mostly members of the Community Church and are working to build a Church School for preschool through fourth grade. We have purchased the land, have an architect who will be ready to work after a while, and we have the funding to complete the building and equip it with the latest and best."

"However, the ladies realize that there will be on-going operating expenses for salaries and upkeep. So they have suggested that Baker House set up a Foundation to accumulate an endowment fund that will produce the necessary income each year. Not only could your Company contribute, but our workers have also suggested that you could exert great influence on many large corporations to also help. So, I guess that's about it. I did not suggest this. It is their idea, but I also think it is fair."

I stopped talking and we sat quietly for a minute. Mr. Whitman pondered the proposal and then responded.

"I should have known I couldn't put one over on you, Angela. Actually, I really didn't intend to do that. I hope you can believe me. I had thought my offer was generous. Now I can see that your ladies are right, of course. But I am the one who will have to convince our Board. We have a couple of penny pinchers who may be a little tough to sell."

"I understand. Just do what you can. Any of us would be glad to make a presentation to your Board if that should be needed. But I think you understand the situation thoroughly."

"I sincerely hope this merger works, because I believe it would be good for all concerned. But if it doesn't, Angela, we aren't any worse off than we were, and we can try something else."

Mr. Whitman pushed back his chair and began to rise. So did I. The discussion was over. Now, we would wait and see what happened next.

~ ~ ~ ~ ~ ~ ~ ~ ~ ~ ~ ~ ~

It was one week later that Mr. Whitman called to see if he could come and make a formal offer to the ladies in our shop. Of course, they agreed.

We met in the lounge early one morning before it was time to open the doors of the show room to the public.

As Mr. Whitman stepped forward, he was carrying a roll of charts and diagrams and I wondered if he was going to "talk over our heads." But not so. Everything was simple and straight forward. Baker House would take our business as it is now, building, equipment, designs, workers, etc. Their label would appear on our productions from now on. They reserved the right to use the name of a particular designer, if they desired.

In return, each person would continue in her present position for now, with a twenty percent increase in salary. Outstanding work would be rewarded with promotions and pay increases.

Baker House had already set aside $1,000,000 in a special fund as a reserve to create a Foundation for the benefit of the Church School. They expected additional funds would be given by other sources.

Then he looked at the women, and smiled. "I believe that covers everything. Now it's up to you. Do you want me to leave while you take a vote?"

"That won't be necessary," Becky spoke up. "You've done everything we asked, and more. There's no way we could turn down your generous offer. We will have to leave all the legal details to you, but as of now, we're working for Baker House. Thank you, Mr. Whitman. We'll make you proud."

I took Mr. Whitman aside. "There is just one thing we need to get straight. Becky Rogers is technically in charge of this business. I gave it a jump start, but she and the friends she has recruited have built it to its present fine condition.

"I may still want to keep my hand in the business now and then. I'm getting married soon and will no longer be a 'free agent', but rather I'll be part of a marriage that will need maintenance and that will come first with me. We have two well-trained and skillful designers who have proven their work already, so you won't miss me. You and I have been friends for many years, Mr. Whitman, and I'm sure you can understand my position now."

"Of course I can. To tell the truth, I was just waiting for something like this. If you hadn't told me, I probably would have suggested it myself. Your work for us, years ago, was outstanding and now you have created a very promising division for our Company. You deserve a rest."

"Our attorneys will draw up the formal papers and the change-over will be painless. Hope you will be around for a while." He shook my hand and left.

I took a deep breath, turned from the workroom, and looked out the window with unseeing eyes.

Chapter Forty-Seven

I sat on the porch swing, drifting back and forth. The night was still. No moon, but the stars were sparkling all across the sky. I tried to imagine the distance from here to there. Impossible. Although they couldn't see me, I could see them, and feel the God who had created them so long ago. How could I have been so blind for so many years? Now the light of God shines in my heart -- not just star light, but the light of His love that sent me a Savior who died for me and saved my soul. The light of his mercy and forgiveness for all the things I had done against Him. The light of his protection and provision.

As I look back down the years to the day I turned my back on Him and walked away, I now see that He didn't give up on me, but continued over and over to demonstrate His great love for me. First, he gave me Chuck, who taught me abut real love; Rusty, the light of my life; great friends; Dad's faithfulness in praying for me; blessing my physical eye sight; providing all the material things I needed; and giving me great opportunities to do things I enjoyed. And then He was so quick to forgive me when I finally came to my senses.

What an amazing Heavenly Father! Of course, there is no way I can repay Him for that love. But I will love Him in return all my life and do my best to show His love to others along my way.

And now -- tomorrow I will marry Michael Kradel, a wonderful man who has also loved me and waited for me to turn back to God. A man who has been a father to Rusty, who has always needed him. A man who is a good and faithful servant for the Lord. And a man I love with all my heart and will try to make happy for the rest of our lives..

~ ~ ~ ~ ~ ~ ~ ~ ~ ~ ~ ~ ~

The girls at work insisted it was their privilege and responsibility to design and make my wedding dress. I trusted them. Gave them complete freedom, yet warned them that if it didn't fit, or I didn't like it, --'Off with their heads!'

I tried it on yesterday and, of course, it was perfect. Made of ivory satin with gold flecks scattered across it. The skirt was street length, flowing gently from the fitted waist. The bodice was form fitting with an oval neckline. A long line zipper in the back insured the perfect fit. The long sleeves were tapered with points over the backs of my hands. The veil, made of the same color net, was attached to a small golden crown. A long, hammered gold necklace, clasp just below the neckline with a large pearl clip was their gift to me. When I looked in the mirror, I was surprised. I really looked like a bride! They did a beautiful job, and I didn't know how to thank them, but they were so pleased with themselves, I don't think they noticed.

I stopped by the church right after lunch to see how things were progressing, and what I saw caused me to hold my breath. The ladies had gathered every flower from their gardens and those of their neighbors. The sanctuary was beautiful.

Becky made the wedding cake and was in charge of the whole celebration.

Her sweet daughter, Jean, was her very capable assistant. My, my, children grow up much too fast. Jean had married just about a year ago.

Hard to believe. But they had everything under control.

All I had to do the next morning was to dress and walk down the aisle on Dad's arm. Dad, Rusty, and Willie would back up Michael. Doris, Betty Jean and Becky would stand with me.

It was like a beautiful dream come true. So I sat for a while, not moving, not really thinking, just feeling at peace. I had walked in the dark far too long.

Almost as if planned, the morning's Devotional passage was from 1 Peter, --"*that ye should show forth the praises of Him who has called you out of darkness into His marvelous light.*"

Epilogue

I was putting the groceries away and thinking how much fun it was to have someone special to cook for. I had lived alone much too long.

It was also great to have someone with whom to share things, someone who was really interested in what I thought or had accomplished, and someone I could lean on, with trust and love. Also it was wonderful to have someone need me, my approval, my opinion, and the comfort of just being together. The past six months have been a whole different life.

The phone startled me. But I was delighted to hear Mike's voice.

"Hi, sweetheart. What are you doing?"

"Oh, Mike. So good of you to ask. I'm putting away the groceries, and planning some goodies for you."

"Hey, I'll look forward to that. Say, do you remember Ted Thomas? I'm sure I've mentioned him to you."

"Yes, dear, if you are referring to Dr Theodore H. Thomas, the most famous gynecologist this side of the North Pole."

"That's the one. Wonderful fellow and great doctor. I would trust him with any of my patients."

"Oh, I'm so glad to hear you say that. It's very reassuring."

"Yes, well, he and his wife, Marie, want to take us to dinner tonight. Think you could handle that?"

"Why, of course, Dear. If you want to go."

"Well, I think his invitation is a nice gesture. We've worked together some, but we seldom socialize. They want to take us to the Golden Slipper. How about that? So, if nothing unexpected happens, I should be home shortly before seven. We are to meet them at eight o'clock."

"I'll be ready, but what should I wear? Is this a real 'dress up' deal?"

"No, I don't think so. Just a nice 'Sunday' dress will be fine. I'll wear that gray suit, with the light blue shirt. If that doesn't suit them, they can send us home to change,"

Mike concluded laughingly.

"Okay, sweetheart. I'll see you when you get here."

~ ~ ~ ~ ~ ~ ~ ~ ~ ~ ~ ~ ~

When we walked into the restaurant, the Thomas' had just arrived. The waiter showed us to a nice table with a view of the orchestra and overlooking the main floor.

There was a little chit-chat until the waiter took our order. As we waited to be served, Marie and I began to get acquainted. Mike and Ted talked shop.

As we were finishing our dessert, Ted turned to Mike and said, "Maybe this isn't the time, but I've got you here, and I wanted to talk to you about a new patient I saw today."

133

"Sure. Sounds interesting. Maybe I'll learn something from the "Great Master.'"

"Well, it's not actually about the case. It's that she said her name was Kradel and she is related to you."

Mike looked very thoughtful, then shook his head firmly. "No, that must be a mistake. All my relatives live back East. I don't know of anyone named Kradel in this area at all."

"Well, she admitted she is related to you only by marriage. Maybe you knew her by a different name. I understand that before her marriage she used the name, Angela Graham."

"What?" Mike exploded! Then he gave me a questioning look.

"Well, you *did* recommend him, dear. I thought you would be pleased."

Turning to me with a very worried expression on his face, Mike asked, "What's wrong, Angela? This man is a fine doctor, but he is a gynecologist. We will find you a specialist --" as his voice trailed off, the light began to dawn.

"Congratulations, old boy! Your wife is about three months pregnant," Ted beamed.

"But, Ted, that can't be. Why, I'm forty-five years old and Angela is forty-two. There must be some mistake."

"No," Ted responded. "All the tests are positive and I have completed my examination. This is not nearly as unusual as you might think. Parenthood isn't just for young people any more. Many couples, older than you, have delivered beautiful, healthy babies. Think of it as a way to stay young -- for at least twenty more years."

Ted chuckled as he patted his old friend on the back. "Some day, we will look back on this and laugh."

"Oh, yeah. Sure." Mike was stunned. I began to be sorry I hadn't warned him.

Suddenly, he looked at me and smiled. "Well, Mom, I guess we had better toddle off to bed. You will need your rest now." And everyone laughed.

After thanking Ted and Marie for a great dinner and good time, we did go home.

To bed -- to sleep -- perchance to dream. We have a future to prepare for.

"I once was lost, but now am found,
Was blind, but now I see."
John Newton
1725 - 1807

Acknowledgements

A big "THANK YOU" to those who have helped put this book in your hands:

Lucille Hodgson, Myra Wells, Cheryl Blevins, and Joan and Charles Baker, and all of you wonderful friends and loved ones who kept cheering me on with your encouragement and support.

Perhaps the young lady, Angela, in the preceding story, never existed. But she lived with me for some time, and I came to understand her feelings, her fears, days of despair, her hopes, her loneliness, and her sorrow for having failed her God for so many years. While I have never denied my Lord in the same way, I too, have failed Him. What a loving and forgiving Heavenly Father.

mc

LaVergne, TN USA
25 March 2011
221615LV00001B/26/P

9 781456 721909